Facing a lonely Christmas Eve, Devin O'Hannigan accepts a stranger's invitation to a private holiday party—hoping to score. But when the merriment takes a bizarre twist, he retreats by himself to call it a night... Until his attention is captured by a teary-eyed Santa in a very short skirt.

Holly's quest to find herself again ends in a disastrous Christmas date, leaving her discouraged and alone in a town far from home. But when her date returns, angry and violent, she's rescued by a gorgeous stranger—the kind of guy she once would have pursued. But that was *before*.

Seeking cheer but preferring anonymity, they embark on an innocent game playing the roles of old friends catching up. Without encumbrances, honest conversations uncover hidden desires. Sparks fly, directing them to an outcome they hadn't expected and shouldn't pursue. But will it thrust them into each other's arms or leave them longing for what could have been?

*Roberta,
Hope you enjoy
my Twisted little
World!*

A twisted little CHRISTMAS

ANNALISE DELANEY

A Twisted Little Christmas
Copyright © 2017 *Annalise Delaney*
Excerpt from *Safe in His Storm* copyright © 2017 *Annalise Delaney*
Print Edition

ALL RIGHTS RESERVED

E-book ISBN: 978-1-948242-00-4
Paperback ISBN: 978-1-948242-01-1

Editing by: Jacy's Red Ink Editing
Cover by: Selfpubbookcovers.com/RLSather and Niki Ellis Designs
Interior Design and Formatting: BB eBooks

All rights reserved. No part of this publication may be reproduced, distributed or transmitted in any form or by any means, or stored in a database or retrieval system, (other than for review or promotional purposes) without the prior written permission of the publisher.

This is a work of fiction. Names, characters, businesses, places, events and incidents are either the products of the author's imagination or used in a fictitious manner. Any resemblance to actual persons, living or dead, or actual events is purely coincidental.

Disclaimer: The material in this book is for mature audiences only and contains graphic content. It is intended only for those aged 18 and older.

Additional disclaimer: While Dominance and submission are very real, this book is fiction and is in no way intended to instruct or teach. If this lifestyle is one you seek, research it, practice caution, and use common sense. Remember that titles don't mean anything until they've been earned and that there are people in the world who seek to take advantage of others. Please educate yourself, and when the time comes, play safe, sane, and consensual.

*To all those
who seek to find their truth.*

ACKNOWLEDGEMENTS

A Twisted Little Christmas was an idea put together in a short amount of time, intended as an introduction to the Perfect Storm series. And although it's not essential to the series—and can be read at any time as a stand-alone—it'll definitely make the rest of the stories all the more fun to read.

I'd like to thank **Kimberly Harris,** who—as always—came through in a last minute scramble to brainstorm and get this idea rolling; **Cari Ferrell,** who offered her time and creative thinking to help me plot it further; **Brooke C, Kimberly Evans,** and **Kimberly Harris** for one of the fastest beta reads on earth; and **Barb Jack,** who helped tirelessly in a last-minute second proofing.

Thanks to **Lorraine Gibson** @ Niki Ellis Designs and **Paul Salvette** @ BB eBooks for their patience with my many questions and requests, as well as their swift attention to designing the book, inside and out!

Many thanks to my dear editor, **Jacy Mackin,** who pushed everything else aside when her sky was falling in order to help get this little story finished and out the door in time for Christmas. My deepest thanks to **Kallypso Masters** for helping me with her experience, referrals, and support, and to **Charlotte Oliver,** who stepped up and took over when my plate was overflowing. Words cannot express my love and thanks.

As always, to my friends and family for their encouragement, cheer, and support—no matter what. Their belief in me kept me going when fear fought to stop me.

You each have my heart and my endless gratitude.

~ Annalise

CONTENTS

Chapter 1	1
Chapter 2	14
Chapter 3	27
Chapter 4	39
Chapter 5	51
Chapter 6	64
Chapter 7	73
Chapter 8	87
Chapter 9	99
Author's Note	109
Sneak Peek *Safe in His Storm*	111

CHAPTER 1

Christmas Eve 2010

DEVIN STUDIED THE hot chick in the driver's seat and wondered how she knew whomever lived at this place. They'd driven about twenty minutes east of the bar where they'd met, and if he knew this area at all, the house hidden behind the thick iron gate wasn't any shack.

After punching in some numbers on the box, the gate opened, and they followed the path around to a large fountain where valets were parking cars. One glance around left him questioning his own attire. People dressed in their holiday best, and he was still wearing the same clothes he'd worn all through his shift. Black on black, it might pass alright, as long as no one came close enough to smell the spilled beer or myriad of other bar drinks he'd no doubt sloshed onto himself throughout the night.

The place was lit brighter than the Fourth of fucking July with all its lights and Christmas decorations. He half-expected to see Chevy Chase from Christmas Vacation come meandering out.

"You good?" she asked.

"Never better." It was a lie, but what was he supposed to say? *Not really, but it's better than being alone at Christmas like some loser?* Yeah, that probably wouldn't go over too well.

The valet took her keys as they exited her badass '69 Camaro SS. "Hurt my car, and I'll have your balls" was what he thought he heard her say to the guy, who Devin studied for a reaction that didn't come. She probably said "job." Whatever. Devin didn't really care since he had no plans to see her or anyone here ever again. This was a simple excursion to pass some time. And have a little fun with the lively girl he met after work tonight.

"So listen," she said as she came around and looped her arm through his. "I was telling you the truth when I said we like to do things a little on the naughty side."

Yeah baby, now she was talking his language.

"So when we enter, there will be this form that they'll want you to fill out before we can go inside."

"A form?" Devin asked, somewhat confused. Was this like a country club or some shit? A place that required membership dues and a bullshit fancy title? He looked around at some of the other guests walking up to the entry. The guys were mostly wearing tuxes, but the women all different kinds of attire. One girl wore a short—a very fucking short—Santa dress, bouncing up the steps. The chick he'd come here with wore tight leather pants and some tall-as-hell boots. In fact, she probably stood taller than Devin in those damn things.

"Yeah," she said, pulling him toward the house. "Just some release forms. Look," she said, pausing and turning toward him. "There's no pressure. But we like to have fun. Sometimes that fun gets a little…interesting. You're not scared, are you?" she asked, using a slightly taunting voice.

"Fuck no," Devin replied, without missing a beat. Damn, maybe this chick wasn't joking when she'd asked him if he wanted to go to a party with whips and chains. "Lead the way, blondie." He couldn't remember her fucking name. Dammit.

She smiled, and something a little wicked lit up her eyes. Devin wasn't sure if it made his dick twitch or his balls hide, but he was down to find out.

They walked up the few steps to a massive entryway and were greeted by an older dude in a tux. Was this guy like a Hugh Hefner? Damn, if he was, Devin was open to making friends.

"Merry Christmas, Madam," he said to blondie. "Sir," he added, nodding to Devin.

Devin offered his hand to shake the older guy's, who appeared surprised but accepted it. "Devin O'Hannigan."

"Edward, Sir," he replied, scanning the list. "May I have the name on the invitation, Madam?" he asked, directing his attention to blondie, now calling her *madam* for the second time. Devin had had a couple beers at the bar earlier, but he wasn't *that* drunk. This chick couldn't be over thirty-five. Why the hell did he keep calling her that?

"Eve Payne."

Eve! That's what her name was! He remembered now because she'd said her full name was Evening, and that's how they'd started talking. Then he chuckled to himself; this chick's full name was Evening Payne? He glanced around to avoid making eye contact. *Some parents are pretty fucked up*, he thought, stifling the laughter that wanted out.

While Edward found Eve's name on the list and exchanged some conversation, Devin took the opportunity to check the place out. They stood in a huge foyer with a high ceiling. A hallway to their left led to a staircase, and he spotted a little coat room off to the side. Straight ahead led to what appeared to be a great room, and he could faintly see their reflection in the long glass window at the farthest end. To his right were three doors, all closed.

"Devin," Eve said, "I just need you to fill these out, and we can head inside. Oh, and he'll need a copy of your driver's license, too."

Devin looked at her. Was she for real? Jesus, maybe they were afraid of people taking off with shit and this was their way of hunting them down if anything went missing. Either way, he didn't steal, so they could have his Costco card if they wanted that, too. He pulled his wallet out and handed Edward his license in exchange for a clipboard.

"Sir," he said while motioning toward a bench. "You're welcome to have a seat while you fill it out, if you'd like."

Devin nodded as he and Eve walked over to the welcome bench. A few more guests arrived, and he noted most of the women were dressed pretty loosely once Edward took their coats. This was an interesting mix of people.

He clicked the pen and began scanning the list. What the hell? Devin swallowed as his eyes travelled over a sex checklist. And holy mother of lucky stars, it wasn't just a sex checklist; it was a fucking kink-o-rama checklist!

A quick look at Eve to make sure she knew what she was getting herself into confirmed that this little vixen was all about it. Devin smiled and began checking things off. A few things seemed a tad extreme, so he didn't bother with them. But if this babe wanted to get tied up and spanked, he was all about helping her out with that Christmas wish.

He finished quickly, and his dick stirred when she smiled in appreciation.

"Shit," he said under his breath.

"What?" she asked, taking the clipboard from him.

He looked around before answering, but to hell with it. Everyone was here for the same reason. "I don't have any condoms with me."

She shook her head and chuckled. "No need. We play here, but one of the rules is no actual sex."

Devin nodded. "Oh okay." He could be cool with that. But fuck, going home with blue balls didn't sound like the best idea, either. Maybe they'd use this for warm-up and could finish off back at her place. Or his. But his was still like forty-five minutes away. Well, no point in worrying about all that now, anyway. If she had some stashed, he could just bang her in her car... Or on it... Or both. After all, nobody said anything about the parking lot being off-limits.

They were shown to the last door on the right, which led into a large gathering room. Dim but not dark, it was illuminated by several wall sconces and chandeliers.

The first thing to catch his eye was the bar, which was set up off to the side and next to an *hors d'oeuvre* table. But that was a given. Devin didn't go anywhere without noticing the bar. Not because he drank, although he liked a cold beer now and again. But because that's what he did. What he had always done, whether or not he'd ever had an option.

O'Hooligan's had been his dad's pub. Pop had opened it up in the little town where they lived, and as soon as Devin had been old enough to wash dishes, that's what he did. Turning eighteen had given him a promotion—and twenty-one an even bigger one. But when Pop died and Devin inherited the place, he got the biggest promotion of them all. He didn't mind being a bar owner. He'd just never been given the chance to choose anything else.

Either way, when he wanted to go sit in a bar and be invisible, he had to drive at least forty minutes to get far enough away to not be recognized. Like he had tonight.

"Can I buy you a drink, blondie?" he said to his escort as they strolled in.

"Well," she answered, "Here's the thing. Due to the nature of what goes on here, there's a house rule of a two-drink max. And my personal rule is only one drink before we play. I find it's better to be in complete control of myself."

He could understand all that. "Cool. So one now and one after?" He nonchalantly adjusted himself. His dick had heard her say the word *play* and gotten curious.

"Sure." She smiled that same wicked grin again. Damn, this chick was a trip. "But let's take a little tour first," she added. "That way we can decide how we want to play."

Fuck yeah. He was ready for tours and more. He didn't even need the drink.

The room they started in had several sitting areas separated by plants and those dressing panels he'd seen in old movies. They were kind of sexy, actually, adding a bit of privacy to each area. Lots of people milled around, talking and laughing, and Christmas music was being pumped in over the sound system.

They stopped at the *hors d'oeurve* table, and he grabbed a couple of bacon-wrapped dates. Turned on by the sexy as fuck way she was watching him, he pressed one gently against her lips.

"Open."

"Say please," she commanded.

"Please." He grew hard when she opened her mouth and licked her lips before allowing him to slide the bite in. She bit onto his fingers before he'd withdrawn them, and her amber colored eyes sparkled when he winced.

"Easy, baby. Let's save the rough stuff for after we're a little more acquainted."

She smiled as she let go of his fingers and chewed the appetizer. He popped his own into his mouth and would have kissed his throbbing finger if it wouldn't have made him look like a pussy.

The bacon-wrapped date was out-of-this-world amazing, and if sex games hadn't been awaiting him, he would have grabbed a plate and piled more onto it. But there was a ton of food here, and he was pretty sure that after they finished playing, he could come back for more.

Looping her arm through his again, Eve led him into another room, adjacent the first.

Well, hello.

Apparently, they'd found the play room. Straps and paddles hung on racks while black toolboxes and some serious looking equipment separated areas of the room. But that wasn't the best part. The best part was that people were in the middle of using this stuff, and evidently, they didn't mind being watched.

Eve leaned over and whispered into his ear. "I'm sure you already know, but just in case," she paused. "There's no interrupting someone's scene. We're cool to observe anyone in here, as long as we're quiet."

Devin pursed his lips and nodded. *Sure. No problem here. Quiet as a fucking mouse. Holy shit, is that guy about to...?*

The dude in front them had his girlfriend strapped spread eagle on some kind of table shaped like an X, and it looked like he was about to smack her pussy with his bare hand. Devin froze, unsure as to whether or not this was cool. He glanced around and assessed that everyone here seemed calm and not at all concerned, so he turned back toward the couple.

"Who's pussy is this?" the guy asked her.

"Yours, sir," she answered—more like whimpered.

"Good girl," he replied, landing a swift smack right against it.

She jerked, but moaned with pleasure. Devin couldn't take his eyes off of them. He'd had the inclination himself to do just that on various occasions, but dismissed those thoughts almost immediately at the time. He had no doubt something like that would have gotten him arrested or, at the very least, thrown out of bed. But damn, this girl was into it.

The guy followed with a succession of little smacks, interrupting just long enough to slide his fingers up through her spread lips and thrust them inside, praising her for being so wet.

Holy shit, where the hell was that drink?

He looked at Eve, who wasn't the least bit uneasy or surprised. She laughed lightly and motioned with her head for him to follow her. Taking him by the hand, she led him past another couple engaged in some kind of rope tying and then a third who were mid-flogging.

He stopped to watch and was amazed at the way the girl seemed completely happy receiving the rhythmic beating from the thick floggers. He didn't know much about this stuff, except for the little bits that he'd seen in skin flicks or heard in locker-room BS, but this was something altogether different than he would have ever expected.

The guy was a master with those floggers, sending them across her body with speed and accuracy. Dressed in merely a bra and panties, her skin glowed pink and she moaned. And in a good way. The kind of moan that always made his cock hard. The kind of moan that said *more*.

"He's really good." Eve's whisper reminded him he wasn't alone.

He nodded. It was pretty clear the guy had lots of practice. "Take long to learn that?"

"For some. But Jake's been doing this since his

twenties."

Devin guessed the guy might have been a few years older than he was. Damn, how the hell long had this shit been around?

"Let's go get that drink." She took his hand, pulling him and his attention away from the attractive couple.

They turned and walked between the few other people who'd gathered to view and headed back out into the main room where it almost looked like any other Christmas Party. Eve stepped in front of him, and as she led the way back to the bar, Devin took the opportunity to appreciate her damned fine ass. The leather pants she wore hugged every curve and valley. He'd been hard for at least the last fifteen minutes, and the current view of those luscious hips wasn't going to slow that down any.

When she reached the small bar, she stopped and patted a barstool, indicating for him to sit. As he approached, she handed the bartender a ticket of some kind and introduced him. "Cole, this is Devin. Would you keep him company while I go powder my nose?" Eve stepped aside so Devin could sit.

"Sure thing, Mistress," Cole answered. "Newbie, huh?" He laughed slightly.

"Seems so." Devin chuckled to himself.

"I'll be right back," Eve said, adding, "and then we can get down to brass balls."

Devin smiled, though not quite sure what the hell

that meant. This chick had a thing for balls, he guessed. Good, he needed his licked. It'd been too fucking long.

Turning his attention to the bartender, he offered a nod. "Give me a Jack and Coke, but hold the Coke."

Cole, the bartender, laughed and grabbed a short tumbler, filling it a little past what he should have.

"Yeah. You've got big ones to take on the likes of her." He nodded in the direction Eve had headed.

Devin shifted on the barstool as he took the glass. "You know more than I do, brother." He downed the liquid in one gulp. "Fuck. Thanks, man," he said, setting the empty glass on the counter. "So what do you know about her? She's a live one, eh?" He grinned, wondering if Cole had tapped her himself.

"Oh, that's one way to put it." He raised his eyebrows as a grin crept across his face.

Devin was beginning to wonder what this guy knew that he probably should, too. "You got a tip?"

Cole looked up and scanned the room. By the way the guy acted, it was probably a good thing they were alone; he leaned in to get the word before the bartender shut up.

"Do everything she tells you, or your balls will ache for days." The guy almost shuddered, like he could feel his own sack aching.

"What?" Devin asked. "Like blue balls cause she won't put out otherwise?"

Cole rolled his head back in a silent laugh. "Seriously, dude, where did she find you?"

A little annoyed, but still in the game, he answered. "Just met her a few hours ago, having a drink. We hit it off, and she asked if I wanted to go to a party with whips and chains. I thought she was joking—but, damn, she was straight up sincere. Anyway, I figured if she wanted to get tied up, I'd be happy to accommodate her."

This time Cole's laugh wasn't silent. After he stopped roaring, he leaned in close to Devin, who was totally confused. "Dude, *she* doesn't get tied up."

Devin looked around. Did she have a friend who did? He'd seen some gorgeous girls here, but they hadn't really even talked to anyone else since arriving, so that seemed unlikely. Turning back to Cole, he swallowed and asked. "So who does, then?"

Cole tapped the mirror behind him, and as Devin followed his finger, his own reflection stared back.

Fuck that.

CHAPTER 2

"Are you messin' with me, man?"

"Wish I was, buddy."

"Holy shit," Devin said, glancing in the direction she'd headed. "Listen, man, that's not my thing. I'm out. Tell her I got a call or something. Tell her I'm in the bathroom. Fuck, I don't care what you tell her, but I gotta jam." He threw a ten on the counter and nodded at Cole as he got his ass in gear and headed back the way he'd come in. Yeah, he was a pussy. But that was better than being someone's bitch.

He passed Edward on the way out, nodded to the guy, and beat feet out the front door. On his way to the gate, he caught sight of a few armed guards in the shadows. Who the hell owned this place? He focused on his objective and saw a walking gate next to the one they'd driven through. A guard shack sat behind one of the brick columns framing the massive iron entry, and inside was another guard and at least a dozen lit up monitors. The security on this place probably cost more than his annual salary.

He reached the gate and paused, making eye contact with the guard.

"Evening," Devin said. "Can I claim a get out of jail free card?"

The guy smiled before punching a button that released the gate. Devin nodded in thanks as he quickly exited, not even turning back to look.

He wondered what the hell made her think he was into that end of things, but holy shit, that was close. Once outside of the gate, he started jogging. There was a long way to go before he'd even reach another main road, so he stopped and tried his cell. Thank fuck, he had service. Ducking into the bushes just in case she came searching for him, he held the phone close to his ear and waited.

"O'Hooly's!" Josie's voice was upbeat and a little out of breath.

"Fuck, Josie—" He paused, trying to figure out where to start and what to tell her. "I need a ride."

"What?" Her reply was loud as other voices and sounds came through the phone. "Sorry, it's really busy in here, and I can't hear you very well. Can you speak up?"

"It's Devin," he said louder. "I need a fucking ride. Who's free?"

Times like these, he wished he had a friend he could call. Once, he had more friends than he could count. High school had been, for lack of a better description, his glory days. But he'd come from a small town in the sticks, and most of his good friends had moved away after high school—either going off to college or getting married and getting out of dodge. He'd stayed around because of the bar. Now, pretty much his only friends were the people who worked for him.

"Hey, Dev!" Josie answered. "No one's free. In fact, I had to bribe Noah to take an extra shift tonight. We're busy as shit!"

He knew the excitement in her voice was due to the fact that it had been slow lately. And normally, he'd be glad to hear that. But right now, he was somewhere in the boonies, hiding in the fucking bushes from a scary woman who wanted to do bad things to his balls.

"Fuck, there's no one?" he said. "What about Gabi?"

"She had a party."

Fuck, fuck, fuck.

"Alright, I'll call a cab," he said. "But if I go missing, you can start looking for me out somewhere by Old Highway 80."

"What?" Josie said. "What the hell are you doing all the way out there?"

"Long story," he answered. "Okay, I'll call you tomorrow."

"'Kay," she said. "Good luck!"

"Shit," he said out loud to no one. He ended the call and opened the browser on his phone, pulling up the nearest cab company, and dialed. "Yeah, I need a ride," he said, eyeing the road for a mile marker or some kind of landmark.

After hanging up, he set off on foot in the direction the cab would be coming from. The farther away he got from Evening Payne, the better.

How in the fuck had he missed all the signs? He picked up his pace into a jog again, ducking out of the way whenever a lone car came from behind him.

Yeah, he was a total pussy. He knew it. But shit, he hadn't been prepared for any of that! He just thought he'd score with a chick who was a little freaky. Which would have been fine if their freaky matched up. But holy mother of fuck me. He had no idea what she had planned and was damn glad he hadn't found out the hard way. That was the one scenario that hadn't even so much as entered into his mind when she'd first mentioned liking things a little on the wild side.

Devin shook his head for clarity, and when an oncoming car with a lit sign on the roof appeared, he raised his hands and waved it down. The cab slowed, and Devin jumped inside, never more thankful to see a cab driver in his life.

"Thanks, man," he said a little out of breath.

"Where to?"

His truck was back at the bar where he'd started, and for a moment, he wondered if she'd come looking for him there. And then he laughed at how much of a scared little girl he was being. Shit, she was just a chick! He should have manned up and waited for her to come back from the bathroom. He could have told her straight to her face that he wasn't into being the catcher, but honestly, at this point, he didn't care anymore. If anything, he was kind of pissed that she didn't tell him what her intentions were *before* she ushered him into a kink party. Either way, he needed to go get his truck, and he damn well needed that drink.

After giving the driver the name of the bar, he sat back in the cab and breathed. As he thumbed through the events of the night, he started laughing. First, he just chuckled, but the more he thought about the pussy way he ran out of there, the louder his laughter grew.

Though quiet, the cabbie eyed him in the rear view mirror, surely thinking he was drunk or stoned or out of his mind. But the dude never said anything, so when Devin paid the outrageous cab fare, he added in another twenty for good measure. The guy'd rescued him, and he was grateful.

"Merry Christmas, dude," he said, handing it over.

"Merry Christmas," the cabbie replied.

Devin nodded, closed the door, and headed toward his truck. It had gotten cold as balls outside, and he'd had enough of this twisted evening. The wind howled, and with it came tiny snowflakes, dissolving the second they hit anything. He looked up and around, wondering if the forecast had been for snow, which was rare at this elevation, but not out of the question.

He pressed the disarm button, opened his truck door, and climbed in.

Rather than head out, he sat there for several minutes, debating what next. He owed himself a damned drink, but the choice was to go home and drink alone like a loser or go to another bar—and drink alone like a loser. Either way, he had no intentions of going to any more parties tonight.

Instead of the same place where he started earlier in the evening, he decided to shed the bad juju and head a little farther down the road to a place he knew would be mostly empty. Why not give the evening a chance to reset itself? He glanced at the clock. *Not even nine yet.* Yeah, he owed himself a do-over.

DEVIN PULLED IN and parked at the High Pine Lodge, shaking off the remnants of his earlier folly. He knew the owners of this place, and if memory served, they were out of town for the holidays, which would mean he could have a drink in the restaurant's tiny bar and not know a soul.

Heading up to the quaint log-cabin lodge, he could see a mostly empty restaurant whose windows lit up the night with a warm, golden hue. The restaurant had a small bar that wouldn't likely be busy since it mostly only hosted guests. And that made it perfect.

Once inside, he scanned the room and its four empty barstools. Choosing the lone stool around the corner of the far end of the bar, he could see the TV better. The volume wasn't on, but it was at least something to distract him. The girl behind the counter didn't appear much older than twenty-one, and he doubted they'd have much to talk about.

"I'll take a bourbon. Neat." He placed a twenty on the counter. "Actually, make it a double... What's your top shelf?" he wondered as she smiled and came walking over.

"Maker's Mark."

He wrinkled his nose, tempted to ask what they considered bottom end; however, the bartender typically had no control over the selection. "Guess it'll have to do."

"Rough night?" she asked with a playful grin.

"You have no idea."

She smiled and turned to get his drink, giving him a moment to glance around some more. Most of the linen-topped tables sat empty, their candles glowing in the center. A young couple with their two kids was just finishing dinner in a back booth, and a lone gray-haired woman relaxed at a table while sipping coffee and tapping on her phone. Exactly the kind of quiet he was looking for.

His drink arrived, and he thanked the girl. The first sip slid down his throat with more burn than he liked. Still, it made the night better. He watched Jim Carrey silently prance around as the Grinch while canned Christmas music hummed through a sound system somewhere.

From the lobby entrance, an older couple walked in, joining the lone woman. Devin observed the trio as they greeted each other with hugs and kisses. They appeared to be family, and that was something he missed.

His mom lived with her second husband in Denver, but getting away to visit her was a chore now that he had the bar to run. Other than his eleven-year-old half-sister, the only other family he had in the states were cousins in South Carolina. He had family in Ireland, but for the most part, he didn't know any of them outside of Facebook.

He and Pop had spent several holidays with Josie's family, and in fact, Devin planned to be there tomorrow. But Christmas Eve had always been spent at O'Hooligans, which just seemed different now.

Of course, sitting at some random restaurant's bar in the middle of nowhere didn't do much to fill the void, but at least he could be miserable without an audience.

He polished off his first bourbon and sipped on the second, deciding he should hang it up and head home once he finished it. There was really no point sitting here feeling sorry for himself.

The restaurant door opened, and a girl came through, causing him a double take. It was the bouncy girl from the kink party, the one in the super-short Santa dress. Only she wasn't so bouncy *now*—wiping away tears.

Devin was immediately annoyed. He'd never liked watching a girl cry—least of all, a pretty one. Worse, something had upset her on Christmas Eve, and that pissed him off even more.

Noticing the other guests, she struggled to pull her skirt lower, although there was little chance it would help—he'd seen the back of that dress at the party, and it showed off some amazing assets.

Staying mostly hidden behind the column, he observed as she approached the bartender.

"Is anyone attending the front desk?" she asked, her voice quivering.

Shaking her head, the bartender explained that the night manager had taken an extended dinner break due to Christmas Eve, but he'd be back in an hour or so. "I'm pretty much in charge until he comes back," she added. "Can I help you with something?"

"My key card," she said. "I left my purse in my…in my date's car. And things didn't work out so well between us." She paused. "I just need to get into my room upstairs."

"Oh," the girl replied from behind the counter, her voice empathetic. "I'm so sorry. I don't have any way into the rooms. If you can wait for Adam to get back, he can handle it, I'm sure."

The pretty strawberry-blonde girl shook her head as more tears appeared. She looked around and leaned in closer, making Devin strain to hear what she said next. "I don't have my phone, my ID, money, or anything," she explained. "I'm only here overnight, and I don't even have a coat to cover up in while I wait."

Nodding, the little bartender reached behind the counter and pulled out a jacket. "It's not very long, but it might help some."

Taking the jacket, Strawberry thanked her and draped it around herself, avoiding eye contact with the older ladies who openly shared some disapproving glances.

"Here," the bartender suggested, "let me clean off that table in the back, and you can wait there. It's kind of private." She came out from behind the bar and headed to the table, wiping it clean and gaining Strawberry's immediate gratitude.

Devin tried to remember who'd he'd seen her with at the party. His first glance at her had been when he'd arrived. She was on her way up the steps and into the house, and he had, quite honestly, been focused on her ass and not her companion.

But then he recalled a big guy taking a drink out of her hand and downing it himself shortly after they'd arrived. Not something he would have probably given a second thought to if it hadn't been for the two drink max rule. That guy had consumed his own two drinks *and* hers.

Something about the girl drew him to her, and he fought with himself to just let it go. He probably shouldn't press his luck with any more women tonight, least of all one who was already in tears. But when he had the chance to finish his drink and bail, he paused, setting the tumbler down nearly untouched.

Wrestling with himself over leaving or not, he saw the bartender pour another drink, smiling when he recognized what it was. A cranberry and cinnamon whisky sour. And she used the good whisky, too. He followed her as she walked it back to the pretty girl in the booth and stood talking to her.

When the restaurant door opened next, a big guy walked in, carrying a purse.

It would have made the perfect opening to a bad joke, and Devin normally would have laughed, but this guy had a pissed-as-fuck sneer and made a beeline straight for Strawberry.

The bartender turned around when she noticed the expression on Strawberry's face, quickly making one of her own as the guy closed the distance across the room. Devin slid off his barstool on instinct as he watched the little bartender step away from the table. Without so much as a word, dickhead grabbed Strawberry by the arm, eliciting a shriek from her and sending Devin sprinting.

"Stop!" she shouted. "I'm not yours!"

"You made a fucking fool out of me," he growled, pulling her out of the booth. "And I don't take kindly to lying little bitches."

"I never lied," she argued, sobbing.

"You—" He didn't finish his sentence because

Devin grabbed him by the shoulder, spun him around, and cracked him in the jaw, sending him stumbling backwards. Hitting the table, he caught his fall and shook his head, dropping the purse and focusing on Devin. "Who the fuck are you?!" he spat, coming toward Devin with a closed fist.

Devin ducked, and the guy missed and spun back around for another go at him. The smell of alcohol wafted off of the fucker as Devin ducked once again. He popped up, turned around quickly, and threw a punch so hard his fist burst with pain on contact. Blood sprayed out of the dude's nose, and he stopped in his tracks, stunned. Taking full advantage of the moment, Devin grabbed the asshole by the collar and dragged him toward the door while he had the upper hand, making a point of accidentally slamming him into the jamb on the way out for good measure.

"Is that your car, fucker?" he shouted, motioning to the only other car parked outside of the restaurant. "Answer!" he added when the guy mumbled.

"Yeah," he answered in frustration and defeat.

"Give me the keys."

"Fuck you," the guy replied.

"Wrong answer," Devin said, throwing him face down onto the car's hood, kicking his legs wide, and pulling his arms behind his back. He reached into the guy's pocket, happy to find the keys without having to dig around. He pulled him off of the hood, walked him the few steps over to the driver's side door, and helped him inside. After Devin reclined his seat, the guy moaned and reached up to touch his nose, apparently finished being a tough guy for the night.

Devin closed the door and tossed the keys under the car, unnoticed.

Looking into the restaurant's windows, he returned the stare of a small audience made up of two older women, an older man, the cute little bartender, and a pretty, strawberry-haired Santa Claus. Shaking his throbbing fist, he headed back inside to deal with what-the-fuck-ever came next.

What a twisted night.

CHAPTER 3

Someone opened the door before he even reached for the handle, and as he stepped inside, he was met with applause from the trio of grandparents. Their snarky looks had been replaced with compassionate ones, and he was glad that had changed, at least. He shook his head and held up his hand, trying to stifle any attention. A guy dressed in a cook's uniform shut and locked the door behind Devin, flipped the sign on the window from *open* to *closed*, and thanked Devin in Spanish.

"*De nada*," he answered, rubbing his fist.

The cook smiled and pointed at Devin's hand. "*Heilo*? Ice?"

Devin nodded, and the guy disappeared into the back. Turning, he accepted a smile and nod from the older threesome who'd settled back into their seats, and he headed in the direction of the girls.

"I'm so sorry," said Strawberry, her voice shaken. "Are you okay?"

"Never better," he answered, wincing when he remembered using the same phrase earlier in the evening. "I'm fine," he amended. "But that guy's gonna have one helluva headache tomorrow."

The girls both laughed, and Strawberry seemed to relax a little.

"I'm gonna call the Sheriff," said the bartender. "I don't want him to wake up and come inside. Or worse, go drive and kill someone. He was pretty drunk."

"One second." Focusing on Strawberry, he asked, "Are you cool with the sheriff coming to get him? Or would you rather he sleep it off? I don't think he'll figure out where the keys are, and I doubt he'll be coming back in here tonight."

Tears began streaming down her face again as she attempted an answer. "This is all my fault," she said through sniffles. "I never should have brought him to that party."

Suddenly, Devin's interest was piqued. *She'd* brought *him* to the party? Was she another dominatrix? She sure didn't strike him as one. Of course, neither had Eve—and all the fucking signs had been there.

"Listen, sweet pea, there's nothing you could ever have done to warrant that. I don't know who that dude is, but he's an asshole. That was not your fault," he finished. "But you need to make the decision on the sheriff." He passed a glance at the bartender, who nodded in understanding.

"Can we just let him sleep it off?" she asked, peering between the two of them. "I'd rather not make his situation worse than I already have."

The cook showed up with a towel wrapped around a bag of ice, and Devin thanked him. Checking the nametag on the bartender, he said, "Let's let things chill a little, Melissa. Okay?"

Melissa nodded. "Okay, but once Adam gets here, I won't be the one making that decision. I need to let him know what went down. Okay?"

Strawberry nodded, and Devin agreed. Melissa left to ring up the trio, who'd decided to call it a night and waited by the register.

"What's your name?" Devin asked.

She glanced up with wide eyes. "I, uh... You know, it's been a crappy night, and I'd really just kind of like to remain anonymous."

A concept Devin understood wholeheartedly.

"Well, unless you want me to call you 'Strawberry' all night, at least give me something."

She laughed. "Strawberry?"

He reached over and gently lifted a curly lock with one finger. "Strawberry."

"Oh, yeah." She blushed. "Okay, why don't you call me Holly?"

Holly. He figured it wasn't her real name, but he'd go with it. "So, Holly, did you check your purse to make sure everything's in it? Or am I gonna have to go back out to that car and crawl underneath for the keys?"

Smiling again, she reached for her purse and

opened it. "Do they pay you for comic relief, or is that a side gig to your job at the MMA?" she asked, thumbing through her purse.

"Side gig," he replied, appreciating her quick wit.

"It's all here." She lifted her gaze to meet his. "Thank you again."

"My pleasure."

When Melissa returned with another drink, Devin realized her first one had spilled during the scuffle. Holly reached for her purse, but he stopped her. "This is on me." He reached for his wallet.

"No," she attempted to reply, but they both were interrupted by Melissa.

"Actually, it's on the house. Would you like another bourbon?" she asked Devin. But he'd had enough to drink and didn't want to be any less sober if the dick in the car did decide to wake up and come looking for round two.

"No, thanks," he said. "But how about a coffee?"

"Sure thing," she answered. "Cream, sugar?"

"Black."

Holly thanked her for the drink, and once Melissa left, he suddenly felt as though he was intruding. "I'm glad you found everything."

She nodded, and Devin stood.

"Oh, you're not going, are you?" Her question sobered him even more.

"I was just going to give you some privacy."

"Actually, I need to go upstairs and change, but I'd

like it if you'd sit and talk for a bit. Let me buy you something to eat," she said. "Have you eaten, I mean?" Shaking her head, she straightened in the booth and rubbed at her arm.

"Actually, I haven't," he said, remembering the single bacon-wrapped date he'd eaten earlier. "Is your arm alright?" He'd forgotten about how she'd been grabbed and now noticed a faint bruise taking form. He offered her the ice he'd been using, his hand feeling better now.

"Oh, I'm okay," she said, shaking her head. "I'll feel better once I'm changed out of this dumb dress."

"I di…don't think it's dumb," he said, almost letting it slip that he'd seen her earlier. He didn't know how to broach that subject considering everything that had happened. But it was probably best not to mention it.

She laughed. "Well, it's certainly not comfortable." She pulled her key card from her purse and scooted to the end of the booth where Devin offered her his hand. "Let me run up to change, and then join me for a late dinner?"

"Only if you were planning on coming back down," he said. "I don't want to be the cause of your missing out on a good night's rest."

She smiled. "Something tells me I'd miss out on more if I called it a night now."

"Okay, then," he replied. "I'll hold down the fort."

"If anyone can, you can." She winked and headed for doorway leading into the lobby. He tried not to stare, but her fish net covered legs weren't an image he'd soon forget.

Devin walked over to the bartop and put down the ice and towel. "Thanks, Melissa," he said. "And can you keep the kitchen open for a few minutes longer?"

She glanced at a clock and nodded. "Few more minutes, no problem."

"Thanks."

He made a quick detour to the head, to both take a piss and reposition his cock. In the few minutes he'd been staring into those glittery green eyes, his pants had become a size too small.

As Devin waited by the doorway for her to return, he kept an eye on the staircase, questioning his own motives. There was no way he'd have let some dude abuse any woman like that. But would he still be hanging around if she weren't hot as fuck?

He didn't even need to answer himself. He knew damn good and well that the answer was a big fat no. He would have been long gone, once he knew the situation was handled. For everything he'd been through all night long, he owed himself a good night's sleep.

But she was more than just hot. She was sweet and sexy and sensual all rolled into a cute little Santa skirt. Seeing her at the party had caught his attention on its own. But realizing what that party was about, he really wanted to find out more about her and what she was doing there.

She'd referred to the oaf as her date, but was he more than that? Devin's interest was piqued, and the fact that the guy was still outside was all he needed to convince himself to stick around.

He tried not to stare as Holly came down the stairs and past the front desk, wearing tight fitting distressed jeans and a fuzzy white sweater. And even though it was bulky, it didn't hide the fact that she was stacked. Her strawberry blonde hair had been pulled back into a ponytail, enhancing her big green eyes and light dusting of freckles.

Not his usual type, but she was fucking gorgeous.

"Feel better?" he asked, greeting her as she stepped into the restaurant.

Nodding, she answered. "More than you know."

He could imagine, but he was willing to feel her for himself to find out for sure. Putting an end to his sick humor, he waited as she handed the jacket back to Melissa, thanking her again.

"No worries," she replied. "But if you guys want anything from the kitchen, I need to order it now."

"Oh, sure." Holly glanced at Devin. "A burger?" That sounded great, so he nodded but took out his wallet.

"No way." She pushed his hand down. "Please let me."

He wasn't raised that way and shook his head no. But something in the look on her face told him she needed to do this.

"Please?" she asked, her voice like honey.

"I don't like it," he began. "But if it's that important to you, fine."

She smiled and pulled out a credit card, handing it to Melissa. "It is. Thank you."

"No. Thank *you*."

When someone began turning the knob to the restaurant door, Holly jumped, catching her breath as Devin moved her behind him. He started toward the door, preparing for round two.

Suddenly, it swung open, and a balding guy in a red sweater vest came through. "Why is the closed sign up and the door locked?" he asked, scanning each of their faces until he settled on Melissa's. Devin stopped in his tracks and turned back toward Holly, who was as white as a ghost.

Fuck, what had that dude done to her earlier?

Melissa came around and explained that there had been an altercation involving someone not staying here, but that a patron had jumped in and played bouncer. She never mentioned who it had been, just that the guy had thrown the keys underneath the car.

Devin took Holly by the hand and led her back to the booth where they'd been sitting earlier, ignoring the glances the manager made as he scanned the room. He'd rather not have to deal with more of that tonight, anyway.

After sitting, he pulled her hand up to his lips and spoke softly. "Let's just look like any other couple on Christmas Eve," he said. "I'd rather not have to explain what happened earlier, if you don't mind."

She smiled and answered quietly. "Ditto."

He kissed her knuckles without thought, and when her eyes lit up, his dick did, too. Which kind of made him a douche, considering he'd been planning on fucking another chick only hours earlier.

Contrary to popular thought, he didn't usually behave like that. Admittedly, he had during high school and the few years after. But he was older now, and it'd probably been at least a year since he'd so much as gotten a blow job.

His potential tryst with Eve earlier in the night had been long overdue and not something he'd gone looking for. She'd been the one to approach him, which was probably why he hadn't picked up on the clues. Sexual frustration could impede a person's ability to make good choices—or so he'd heard. But he decided to put the incident with Eve to rest, once and for all.

"What's your name?" she asked, making him feel like a douche for kissing her hand.

"Devin O'Hannigan."

"Well, Devin O'Hannigan, you just might have won my heart."

His cock rubbed against the inside of his pants

zipper, thickening as she held his gaze. He'd never before wanted to win anyone's heart, but hers he might be interested in.

"I know it's none of my business," Devin said. "But what's your relationship to that guy?" He probably shouldn't have asked her, but curiosity was winning out.

Looking down, she pulled in a deep breath and answered. "We met a few months ago," she said. "This was actually the second time we'd dated. Everything went fine the first time." Her voice held defeat. "I don't understand what happened."

"Well, people aren't always what they make themselves out to be," he offered, not knowing what else to say.

"Yeah," she replied. "I guess I missed the signs."

He completely understood. But before he could reply, they were distracted by a red flashing light. They each glanced outside and saw that the sheriff had pulled up next to the car where her date was sleeping it off.

"Shhh," he gestured to Melissa, who nodded and winked, letting him know she had his back.

They watched as the sheriff tapped on the window and shone a flashlight into the car. When the door finally opened, Devin released the breath he'd been holding. Thank fuck that guy was still alive or he would have a shit storm on his hands. Adam, the night manager, walked outside and talked to the sheriff while the big guy sat in the back of the cruiser. Pretty soon, a tow truck showed up and hooked up the guy's car. And thankfully, not once did anyone come asking questions of them.

As the situation wrapped up, Devin felt a tiny bit guilty until an image of Holly's bruise threw that right out the window.

"Hey, guys," Melissa said, switching the bar lights out. "You're welcome to hang in here, but I'm heading home. Or, if you'd rather, there's a couch and a fireplace in the sitting room. The one with the Christmas tree." She pointed past the front desk and beyond the staircase where Devin could see the lights from a Christmas tree flickering.

He and Holly shared a glance, and when she smiled and nodded, he slid out and helped her to her feet.

"It's late," he said. "Please don't feel like you need to entertain me. Now that your date won't be a problem, I can take off and let you get some rest. Tomorrow's Christmas, and you probably have places to be."

Though she recovered quickly, Devin saw her expression fall. "No," she said. "It should be me letting you get back to your own life." Looking around, she forced a laugh. "I'm sure you were probably just trying to enjoy a few minutes of quiet until all of this completely hijacked your Christmas Eve. God, I'm so embarrassed," she continued. "You must have people waiting for you, and instead, you're here babysitting me."

"No one's waiting for me," he answered soberly. "And I don't mind babysitting you."

She smiled as they stood only inches apart, neither moving. Studying her delicate features, he made note of her pert little nose and high cheekbones. And as he stared into her pretty green eyes, he fought the incredible urge to kiss her.

CHAPTER 4

"I'D REALLY RATHER not go up just yet," Holly said softly, finally breaking the silence that had lingered between them. She'd given him her stage name. The one she used when she'd done some singing and acting a few years earlier. The one she had used this evening at the BDSM party she'd been invited to. Some people used their real names, but she didn't think that was a good idea. Even here with Devin, she'd be gone tomorrow and all of this would be nothing but a faded memory.

He stared back at her, his deep blue eyes captivating. His dark hair had gotten ruffled in the altercation earlier, but it enhanced his features, making him appear incredibly sexy.

She probably should go up. Her night had started with one horrible failure, and the last thing she needed to was to make another mistake. But before she could recant her statement, he answered.

"I'd rather not go home, yet."

A moment of silence hung between them as they continued to stand there, frozen in time. Neither comfortable nor uncomfortable, it was simply present.

He took her by the hand and led her in the direction of the sitting room. As they passed the wooden staircase, he looked up. If he'd been thinking about taking her upstairs, he didn't act on it. They entered the room illuminated only by the golden flickers of a fireplace and the multi-colored twinkling lights of a Christmas tree.

She knew the warmth spreading over her came both from the fire and the ambiance. Something was very comforting about being in a room lit by fire, but when a Christmas tree was added in, the combination was like no other.

After seeing her to one of the cushy couches, Devin walked to a nearby antique buffet set up as a self-serve coffee station. He pulled out two mugs and filled one. "Hot chocolate?" he asked. "They have tea and coffee selections, too. But I've never known a girl who didn't prefer hot chocolate next to the tree on Christmas Eve."

Holly smiled. "I'd prefer brandy, but hot chocolate sounds perfect."

"Brandy, eh? I could probably sneak back into the bar..."

She laughed openly. "No, that's quite alright. Avoiding the sheriff once tonight is probably as lucky as we'll get."

"So where are you from?" he asked, stirring her cocoa.

She paused, considering her situation. Wasn't that

the million dollar question? Everything in her life was amidst change, and she couldn't have answered him honestly if she'd tried.

"Would it be terribly rude to not answer that?" she asked.

He turned and cocked his head to the side as a sly smile crept up one corner of his mouth. "I've never heard of that. Is it in California?" he teased, handing her the warm mug and setting down his own.

Appreciating his humor, she replied, "As a matter of fact, it is."

"I'll have to visit there sometime," he said, holding his mug up in toast.

She smiled and looked down, noticing his still-swollen hand. "I'm sorry," she started. He'd come to her rescue earlier and had been kind enough to babysit her for the last couple of hours. Didn't she at least owe him some normal conversation? But how could she even begin to explain? "My life is in the midst of something right now. This," she motioned around with her hand, "was supposed to be a...a different kind of night. Everything about this trip was set with the intention of getting away and trying to find myself again." She paused, already saying more than she wanted to. More than he cared about or needed to know. "Can I just be Holly from Anywhere, USA tonight?"

He studied her for a minute before answering. "Sweetheart, you don't owe me anything. You can be anyone you want to be with me, as long as you're honest in what you do say." His eyes twinkled when he smiled, and even though his statement was comforting, she still wished she had more to offer him.

"What you did earlier," she began, "could have saved me from something terrible. If I haven't thanked you properly, I am now."

"What I did was necessary, and I'm glad I was here. He didn't seem fazed by assaulting you in public. Guys like that are nothing but trouble."

She nodded. He was right, and had she listened to her inner voice, the night would have gone differently. "I know," she said. "And I'm sorry my lack of judgment caused you any pain." She ran her hand gently across the back of his, willing the swelling and pain away.

When he shifted and reached for the mug, she withdrew her hand, reminding herself that not everyone appreciated being touched by a damned stranger. She couldn't help herself, though. It was her nature to nurture. To touch. And to love.

"Where did he come from?" Devin asked, interrupting her thoughts. "You'd mentioned something earlier about him not being who you'd thought." She didn't remember telling him that, though it had been the truth. And she did want to be as honest with him as she could, despite withholding her identity.

"We met online a few months ago," she explained. "We spoke daily and eventually decided to meet. The first time, we met near where I live, attending a party thrown by a friend. This time was my turn to travel." Her mind drifted to the weekend they'd first met. There had been signs, but she'd ignored them, chalking it up to nerves on his end. "Anyway," she continued, "not all people are who they pretend to be."

"In my estimation, most people aren't who they pretend to be," he said, laughing.

"You don't have to tell me, but what do you do?" she asked.

"I'm a shrink, a bodyguard, and occasionally a superhero," he said, his eyes twinkling again when he smiled. "And I like your idea of remaining somewhat anonymous," he added. "It takes all the pressure off, and we can sit here and talk candidly. No judgments. No pressure. No bullshit. Just two people opening up and being real."

She pondered the invitation. How different would it be to meet someone for the first time and simply feel free to share all your secrets without the worry of being judged? The thought fascinated her as did getting to know as much about him as she possibly could in a single, anonymous evening.

"I have an idea," she said.

AS LONG AS it didn't involve putting him in bondage, Devin was open. "Oh?" he asked, appreciating the way her eyes lit up when she'd thought of something. "Shoot."

"Well," she began. "We used to do something in Drama to get to know each other."

He couldn't stop the image that suddenly flashed through his mind of her playing Santa in *The Grinch*. But when his dick pepped up once again, he tried to focus on something other than the way her perfect ass cheeks peeked out from under the skirt she'd worn earlier.

Shit, he needed to get rid of this damn hard on. "Okay," he said, nonchalantly reaching for his coffee, hoping to relieve some of the tightness against his cock. "I'm game."

In her excitement to share, she didn't appear to notice his awkward positioning. His appreciation for the dimly lit room suddenly increased.

Her body language said so much more when she slipped out of her shoes and pulled her feet up onto the over-sized sofa they shared. Getting more comfortable, she mindlessly pulled one of the throw pillows into her lap as she began explaining. Her smile deepened, and her eyes stayed lit.

"We would take turns asking a personal question and go around the room, each one of us answering it."

Devin nodded toward the empty room. "Seems like a pretty short game."

She swatted him with the pillow and laughed. "Oh, stop," she joked. "It's perfect for this. We can totally stay anonymous, but we have to answer all questions honestly. Come on. It'll be fun. And like you said earlier, no judging. No pressure. No BS. Just two people getting to know each other."

Why the fuck wouldn't his dick go to sleep? And what the hell had he gotten himself into? "Sounds good," he answered while his conscience shot him the WTF face. "Who starts?"

"Well," she said, snuggling the pillow again. Devin watched as a soft ringlet fell loose from her ponytail at the side of her face. "I guess I will. And we should probably make it a rule to try and keep the personal questions unrelated to identity."

"Aren't they *all* going to be personal questions?" He smirked.

A grin spread across her gorgeous lips. "I suppose so."

"Okay, then," he said. "So if it's too personal, we'll say 'new question.' Sound good?"

"Sounds good," she said. Then narrowing her brows, she seemed to study his face. "How old are you?"

He smiled. This game was gonna be a breeze. "Thirty."

"Okay," she said, smiling. "Your turn."

His cock had a question for her, but since his cock was in time-out, Devin ignored him. "Same question. How old are you?"

"Thirty-one," she said. "So respect your elders."

He laughed. "Goofball."

"Did you grow up around here?" she asked next.

"Somewhere around here," he said, maintaining their agreed anonymity.

"Right," she replied, a sly smile crossing her lips.

"How long were you in Drama?" he asked, drifting slightly from the boring getting-to-know you questions.

"Oh," she answered, perking up again. "All through high school and college."

Nodding, Devin sipped more coffee and waited for her question.

"Where'd you learn to fight like that?" A slow smile crossed her lips, and her eyes did that twinkling thing again.

"All through high school and college." A smug grin pulled at the corner of his mouth. "It comes in handy for my superhero job."

She rolled her head back in a silent laugh.

"Was this game this much fun in Drama?" he teased her.

"Well, we *were* kids!" She grinned, emphasizing the word.

"We aren't kids now," he said, his tone growing serious. When she adjusted her position, Devin put his hand on her knee. "We're old friends," he prompted. "We don't need to ask all those questions because we already know the answers. We're catching up with each other after a few years of not seeing one another.

No one's nervous. No one's judging. We're just happy to see each other again and have one night to catch up."

Her eyes softened as she listened to each word he spoke. Her shoulders dropped, and she settled comfortably into the couch again, the way she had before the questions started.

"So comfy friends then?"

"That's right, Strawberry. Old comfy friends."

Nodding, she smiled. "So have you been dating anyone?" Her tone held apprehension.

Devin sat back and settled into his corner of the sofa. "Not since last year," he answered honestly. "Work keeps me so busy I sometimes forget what it's like to date."

Her head tilted and the subtle smile she wore sent warmth throughout his body and soul. It was an interesting thing to watch another human being's expressions and know what they were thinking even when words were absent. And right now, he'd bet ten bucks she was feeling empathy.

"Not even an occasional date?" she asked, out of turn.

"No." He grinned without explaining. "And that was two questions, so now I get to ask two in a row."

"Okay." He noticed when she appeared to brace herself slightly.

"What attracted you to the asshole from earlier?" He jumped in with both feet. The guy was average-looking, probably a few years older than her, and didn't seem to be the type he'd expect her to go for.

Her mouth opened as she took in a breath, but she didn't shift, so he relaxed and waited for her to answer.

"I..." She directed her eyes into her lap, inhaled deeply, and started over. "The truth is, I've been living a lie for the past five years," she started. "Thinking I could be someone I'm not. Which was my first mistake and, no surprise, didn't work. I guess I was so hungry to find myself again that I settled for the first guy who appeared to compliment that." She paused, but Devin waited. There was more, and he wanted to give her plenty of opportunity to say it. Another moment passed, and she shifted slightly, tucking her feet under her butt and hugging the pillow. "It was a foolish thing to do, and I realize that now. The signs were there, but I guess I just saw what I wanted to see." She lifted her eyes to meet his. "I can't make the same mistake again."

They held each other's gaze, and Devin realized he was seeing well past the mask she'd had on earlier and directly into her soul. How many women other than Josie—and occasionally Gabi—had he ever seen this candidly? He couldn't think of any.

"Everyone's entitled to a one-time pass," he said. "Don't beat yourself up over trusting the wrong person—it happens. But that's not my question," he said, draping his arm on the back of the sofa. He studied her, intent on getting to know her as much as possible in the little time they had together.

"You said you lived a lie. That you weren't true to yourself."

She nodded. "I did. But that's not a question."

"No," he continued. "So tell me, what does being true to yourself mean?"

Her expression remained controlled. In fact, she sat up just a little straighter before she answered. "It means I'm done hiding who I am and what I need. I'm done pretending to fit into the mold society wants me to fit into. I know who I am, and I know what I need."

That wasn't the answer he'd wanted; however, the flaw was probably in his question. But now she'd given him the perfect one.

"Are there things you hide, Devin?" she asked, her voice liquid honey. "Things about yourself no one else knows? That no one would suspect? Or worse, things that would make them see you differently?" Her voice had grown sensual, almost seductive, as she spoke. And when she stared into his eyes, he felt a connection that made him weak.

"We all have things we hide," he answered as images flitted through his mind. "I don't know if any of my secrets would make people see me differently, but it's a good question. And one I'd have to give more thought to if I wanted to be honest."

She smiled. "Then I'll take a rain check on the

answer."

"Deal," he replied, glancing out the window and seeing that the snow had begun to collect on the ground and cars. He drew his attention back to his real interest and focused on her beautiful green eyes. "You said you know who you are and what it is you need," he said. "So I want you to tell me. What is it you need, Holly?"

CHAPTER 5

SOME PAUSES SEEM longer than others, and this was one of those times. Convinced she needed to talk, he wanted to listen. So he waited.

"I need to be manhandled," she finally said. "But in a way that reminds me I'm valued. I need to feel powerless. But in a way that makes me feel protected. I need to feel dominated. But in a way that lets me be free. I need to be held down and fucked hard," she said bluntly, gaining the attention of his now-throbbing cock. "But by someone who can handle the responsibility of everything else. Someone who can offer me a lifestyle that caters to an exchange of power. But not the kind you saw in the restaurant earlier. *That*," she emphasized while touching her bruised arm, "was straight up abuse." She paused, and Devin remained poker-faced, despite the renewed urge to beat the shit out of the guy all over again. "I need someone to be accountable to. Someone I respect. Someone who understands consent. You asked me what I need, but before you can understand that, you need to understand who I am. *What* I am," she added. "I'm a submissive, Devin. Someone who requires a certain lifestyle. And to be true to myself, I need a Dominant."

It was the most real conversation he'd ever had with a woman. With *any* woman. She was pouring her heart out, and even though he didn't deserve her trust, he was overcome with an insurmountable sense of protecting it.

This explained her presence at the party earlier. The terminology was new, but he was beginning to understand what she was explaining. Sadly, it made him look like a huge dickhead for his personal reasons for being there. He'd gone to score. Period. Forget the fact that he would have been painfully enlightened had he stayed. His true motives now made him feel like a complete asshole. He considered telling her about being at the party, but saw no point. She might see him differently, and he wasn't ready for this to end yet. She wasn't like anyone he'd ever known, and he was just beginning to adore her.

"TMI?" she asked after a stretch of silence.

Devin leaned forward, reaching for the lone curl and tucking it behind her ear. "Not in the least," he answered honestly. "That was truly the most honest conversation I think anyone has ever had with me. Thank you for trusting me enough to share yourself like that."

Holly nodded, but her expression remained neutral, and Devin wondered if she regretted sharing as much as she had. There was still more complexity to this small framed girl that he wanted to uncover. "I'd really like to know more," he said, appreciating the way her expression relaxed. But the conversation had become heavy and required an intermission. "So we're not finished yet," he said, adding, "Not even close. But before it gets too late, I have another idea."

She tilted her head apprehensively until Devin pointed outside. "Do you have a warm jacket and boots?"

Turning toward the window, she slid off the couch and stood up. "Oh my gosh, when did all of that happen?!"

Damn. Her smile was something he might never get enough of. "In the past couple of hours," he said. "It'd started earlier, but hadn't been sticking. I guess it finally got cold enough."

"Yes!" she squealed. "I never see snow! I'll run upstairs and get my coat." She tossed the pillow onto the couch and grinned. "Wait, okay?"

"Of course," he teased. "It was *my* idea." He winked, and she turned to dash up the stairs.

Devin re-warmed and added plastic lids to their hot drinks, wondering how late she'd let him keep her up. It was anyone's guess what her plans were for tomorrow, and he really couldn't ask. They were sharing an anonymous evening, and those questions were off-limits.

As he waited for her to return, he realized that if Eve had been who he thought she was, he'd probably be fucking her somewhere right now. And that thought actually made him sick. He would have never ended up at the lodge and would never have met Holly. At least not like this. And even though this night wasn't going to end in sex or go anywhere tomorrow, it was the best Christmas Eve he could remember having.

"What about you, Superman?" she called from behind him. "Do you have a warmer jacket or is your cape enough?"

Laughing, Devin turned around to face her. "Both are in the truck. But I'll settle for the coat," he said, winking. "I think the cape needs a break for the night."

She giggled and came bouncing over, taking the cocoa he offered. "Oh, it's warm," she said, tilting her head again. "Thank you."

He gestured toward her mittened hands and said, "You really did come prepared."

"Ha!" She laughed. "You don't know how badly I was hoping it would snow." Her eyes lit up, and she clapped her hand against her thigh. "It never snows where I live, and this has been on my bucket list."

"Then let's go check it off," he said, completely taken by her charm. They exited the cozy room and passed by the front desk, nodding to Adam, whose head popped up from his tablet long enough to nod in reply. As they opened the lobby door, they were met with a blast of bone-chilling air.

"Fuck," Devin said, pulling Holly against his side for warmth. Leading her toward his truck, he quickly opened the door and set his coffee on the floorboard. After grabbing his heavy coat from behind the seat, he noticed she was shivering and retrieved a beanie and scarf from the center console. "Here," he said, taking her paper cup and setting it next to his.

He tugged the beanie over her head and wrapped the scarf around her neck and mouth, covering half her face.

"Wow, thanks." She laughed, adjusting it and tucking in her hair. "It's freaking freezing out here!"

"Yeah," he agreed, quickly shrugging on his coat, adding gloves he pulled from the pocket. "But now we're committed," he teased as the wind blew snowflakes against their faces. "Let's come back for the drinks."

She nodded, and Devin closed the door, pulling her against his body once again, appreciating the way she fit.

They set off down the path that led around the lodge. Old oak trees were lit with miniature light strands wrapped around their trunks, illuminating the drifting snow as they passed each one. His ears were freezing, but knowing she was wearing his beanie gave him a different kind of warmth. And his dick had no idea it was under thirty-two degrees out. In fact, *he* was having his own little summer.

Holly shivered as they pushed down the path, both

freezing. And then she started to giggle. Devin turned and watched as her laughter grew into the belly-hurting kind. "What's so funny?" he said, snickering himself now, merely because she was.

Raising her voice in order to be heard over the gentle howl of the wind, she fought back her amusement and shook her head, wiping at tears that were nearly freezing on her cheeks. "This wasn't what I dreamed of!"

Unable to resist her incredible cuteness, he pulled her closer and wrapped his arms tightly around her, shielding her from the blowing wind. She nuzzled her face into his chest for warmth, and he fought to dismiss the carnal thoughts playing in his mind.

"Not what you thought, eh?" He chuckled, pulling her back and peering into her face. Her cheeks were bright pink, and he couldn't help but smile.

"Not exactly," she answered, offering him a pathetic expression.

He shook his head, teasing her. "O-kay," he said, sounding crushed. "We'll just go back in where it's warm." He turned away from her and began to walk in the direction they'd come, adding, "*Rookie.*"

Grinning to himself, he got about three steps away when suddenly a child-sized snowball hit him on the back of the head.

HOLLY WATCHED AS Devin turned around, hoping he'd

laugh. She probably shouldn't have thrown a snowball at him, but she couldn't resist. Plus, a snowball fight was on her bucket list, too, and this might be the only chance she'd ever have. So no bone-chilling, cold-as-a-witch's-tit snowstorm was getting in her way.

The look on his face was priceless. Until it was replaced with a wicked grin. When he put down his cup and reached to scoop up some snow, she turned and ran. That damn snow was cold! No way did she want to—

Thump!

"Holy crap!" Even through her jacket, she could feel the chill against her arm. "Hey!" she said turning around. "I only threw a baby snowball!"

Thump!

He threw another right as she was talking! "Oh!" she yelled as she watched him bend to scoop up even more. "You play dirty!" Darting around the corner, she hid behind a tree, scraping up as big a hunk as she could get, smashing it firm while she waited for him to appear.

As soon as he came around the path, she heaved it toward him, nailing him right in the shoulder. He glanced to the side, spotted her, and lifted his eyebrows.

"You're the devil!" she spat, turning to run again.

"You shouldn't start fights you can't possibly win," he warned, now stalking even closer.

She heard him chuckle while she jetted farther

down the tree-lit pathway to the far back of the lodge. Her face was freezing, but her adrenaline pumped so hard the cold was barely noticeable. It was an odd blend of sensations, but she loved every bit of it. Another snowball came in her direction, hitting a tree. She looked back and stuck out her tongue, his distance giving her more confidence than it should have. Because that's when he stopped walking and started jogging. Right. For. Her.

"Ahhhh!!" she yelled as she turned to get away, changing course and heading off the path. Gaining a mere few feet, the ground dropped away, and she lost her balance, sinking into snow as the ground sloped. Suddenly, strong arms wrapped around her and pulled her back, saving her from sliding down the embankment into the dark.

"It's cold as balls," he growled, setting her steadily onto her feet. "And you're out here running right into trouble!"

Laughing hard, she only caught her breath long enough to squeak out an answer. "But it was on the list!"

"What? Sledding into a trench in the damn dark?" he asked.

"No," she teased. "A snowball fight!"

"Well, you weren't gonna be any good down there." He gestured with his gloved hand toward the gully she almost wound up in. "Is getting a spanking on your damn list, too?" he added, his tone slightly annoyed.

Turning into him, she lifted her gaze and met his. "No, sir," she said without thinking.

When he cocked his head slightly, a small smile appeared before she averted her gaze, embarrassed. He wasn't a Dominant, she reminded herself. But the words and tone he used were enough to grab her attention. And awaken her submission.

"Come on," he said, taking her by the hand. He guided her out of the snow-covered rough and onto the smoother, powdery walkway. "It's too cold out here, so if there's anything more on that list, rest assured it's not happening outside tonight."

She followed him, completely sucked into the role he'd assumed, whether or not he was even aware. Devin was the kind of guy she always fell for. Tough, insanely attractive, and too charming for his own good. The problem was, they always ended up being players. Boys who acted tough but didn't have the 'nads to back it up when real life came around and brought surprises.

They reached the front door, and as he opened it, she halted her thoughts, scolding herself for making assumptions about him. That wasn't fair, and none of it mattered anyway. He wasn't a Dom. He wasn't her date. He wasn't her anything. He was her made-up, long-time friend. The one she'd vomited her life's mission statement onto earlier, lucky to find him still listening after she'd finished. The least she could do was honor her own words and stop trying to judge him at all. Especially when comparing him to men who'd done nothing but disappoint her. He'd been a gentleman all night.

Holding the door open, he pulled off a glove with his teeth, waited for her to enter, and—

Thwak! He swatted her right on the ass.

"Owww!" Heat spread across her stinging butt, and before she could even turn to face him, his hand made contact with her other cheek, duplicating the sensation. She yelped a second time, suddenly realizing that Adam was staring directly at them, his hand holding a sandwich, his mouth in mid-chew.

"That was for almost getting both of us skewered by shit hidden in the shrubbery."

"Are you kidding me?!" she blurted out, covering her butt and whipping around in his direction.

"No," he said, calmly, following her into the lobby. "If you can't see what's under the snow, you have no idea what lurks there."

Shooting him an incredulous smirk, she lowered her voice. "That's not what I'm talking about, and you know it."

He had the audacity to smile. That charming, wicked, evil smile that she should run from.

Now. Right now.

But instead, she narrowed her eyes and bit back

the laughter threatening to replace her hard-earned scowl.

"I think we should take our discussion to a more private area." He gestured toward Adam who was enjoying a snack while watching them. "Dinner and a show," Devin whispered in her ear. And that was all it took. She burst out in a spit and a guffaw, setting off an uncontrolled, unladylike pattern of giggles.

Grabbing her mittened hand, Devin led her away from the night manager's view and into the sitting room. Her laughing calmed when he pulled off his remaining glove and then removed her mittens, briskly running his hands over them.

"I can't believe you did that," she said, watching his hands warm hers.

"Which part?" he asked, that boyish devil-smile back.

"All of it. Any of it. What kind of friend *spanks* another?" she asked, her tone sarcastic.

Devin stopped rubbing her hands and eyed her. "The kind that knows the other one needs it."

A wave of need washed over her, melting the chill left from the snow. He wasn't a Dominant, she was sure of it. But what was this? Instead of answering, she opted to let it go. They still had time to chat, but right now, she was cold, and her jeans were wet.

"I need to change," she said. "I got all wet trying to hide from you." Her own thoughts immediately slid straight into the gutter with her last sentence. She averted her eyes, looking away when he didn't.

"I like you wet."

Well, snap.

Glancing back, he grinned and winked. "You know I'm just playing with you, right, Strawberry?" He pulled off the beanie she wore, her hair falling around her face, her ponytail holder hardly doing its job. "I should probably go," he said, taking a step back. "Before you kill me. Or at the very least," he added, "hate me."

Her hand shot out and grabbed him by the arm, stopping him. "I don't—"

Again, she found herself staring into his eyes, words absent. Somewhere in the distance, a grandfather clock began chiming, and as it bonged, she counted them off, one by one. His deep blue eyes twinkled as they moved over her face, searching for something. Her breath became shallow as she followed his eyes. Her heart raced, and her eyes grew heavy.

On the twelfth and final bong, Devin's lips slanted across hers, and she opened to him with total surrender. He swept into her mouth, tempting her tongue to dance, and it did. They found a common rhythm, and her heart pounded as her body soared. It'd been so long since she'd felt small and taken. Too long. And as the kiss deepened, her body was pulled against his, where she fit like a glove. When one of his hands slid into her hair and held her firmly, she nearly moaned.

Did he know she liked her hair pulled?

Finally, he slowed, and as their mouths parted, she opened glassy eyes and was consumed by his.

"Merry Christmas," he whispered. "But our time's up."

CHAPTER 6

"No," she said, her voice sincere. "I mean, if you have to go, then yes. But you said no one was waiting, so if no one is…" She seemed to struggle with her words, finally ending with, "I'm not tired."

Devin smiled, his lips still wet with the taste of her kiss. He didn't want to go, either, but it was getting late, and he didn't want to test his luck much more. He'd already pushed the envelope when he'd smacked her on the ass. But now he'd crossed the line and kissed her. Friends didn't kiss like that. And he was so hard he wasn't sure he could keep himself from pushing that envelope all the way to the mail box.

Plus, they'd garnered the attention of the dude in the red sweater vest who totally fit the profile of creepy peeper. And since Devin's buddy owned the place, he didn't really want to gain any more attention than he probably already had. Still, she was incredibly hard to resist, and right now, she was pretty irresistible.

"What do you want, Holly?" he asked. She seemed to take well to direct questions, and he was a fast learner.

"I want more," she said softly. "I want to get to know you a little more."

Tipping his head to peer back in the direction they'd come, he looked to see if they had a voyeur. "What if we have an audience?" he asked against the side of her head, breathing in a delicious whiff of her shampoo. Some kind of strawberry, maybe. He wasn't sure, but he'd be happy to guess again. "I don't know about you, but I don't want to be the subject of any creepy you-tube peeper shows," he joked, breathing in another whiff.

Yep, strawberry. How fitting.

She laughed softly and lifted her chin to meet his gaze. "I don't care," she said. "We can sit here and talk, and if he wants to listen, he can listen."

Devin nodded. "Okay, then you run up and change into something dry," he paused, "and warm. When you come back down, I'll have new drinks ready."

Nodding, she turned and headed toward the stairs. "Perfect. Only, coffee for me this time, please," she said as he watched her take the first two steps. "Two creamers and three sugars?"

"Decaf," he amended, ignoring her scoff and heading toward the coffee area. He wasn't going to be responsible for another caffeine-induced jog around the property in a freaking blizzard.

He pulled out his phone to check the time and saw

a message notification. Tapping the icon, his screen lit with a message from Josie.

> **JOSIE:** *You make it out okay?*
> **DEVIN:** *Yeah, called a cab. Thanks*

He should have texted her earlier, but he'd been so caught up in everything he'd completely forgotten. After he made their new drinks, he noticed the fire had died down. Thankfully, a few extra logs waited on the hearth along with some fireplace tools, and by the time he heard the next incoming text notification, he had it stoked and crackling again.

> **JOSIE:** *Don't get too drunk. Momma made your favorite pie*
> **DEVIN:** *Never too drunk for your mom's cooking*
> **JOSIE:** *Good. See you tomorrow, Dev. Merry Christmas! Xoxo*
> **DEVIN:** *Thanks sweetheart. Merry Xmas to you too ;)*

If he'd ever had anyone close to a sister, it was Josie. She was the one woman who'd stuck by his side through every up and every down. He owed her more than he'd ever be able to repay. But that was the thing about Josie; she didn't keep score.

Devin was glad he hadn't ended up shagging Eve, regardless of the circumstances. The entire choice to leave with her had been on pure impulse and not one of his finer decisions. He was beyond thankful it'd turned out the way it had, because regardless of meeting Holly, screwing Eve would have been something he'd regret tomorrow.

The thought brought him back to Holly and question his true motives.

Was he still here because he wanted into her pants? Because, duh, he did. He'd be a fool not to. But was that something he was still hoping for after she'd made it clear she wanted his friendship only—despite the hot-as-fuck-kiss he'd just gotten?

She'd already been abused once tonight. Made to feel cheap and humiliated publicly by the asshole she'd come to town to see. Undeserving fucker. And then there was Adam who ogled her every time she walked past the front desk. Holly probably got that everywhere she went. The last thing he should be doing is hanging out for the wrong reasons. She deserved so much more than that.

He stared out into the darkness, watching the snow fall. Coming to a decision, he walked over to the coffee table, set down her coffee, and took one look back up the staircase. He might be a douche for what he was about to do, but he didn't want to have any more regrets tonight.

Pulling on his jacket, he headed for the front door.

QUICKLY SLIPPING INTO some yoga pants and a sweatshirt, Holly grabbed the brush and smoothed out her tangled locks, securing them with a new ponytail holder. She slid into some fuzzy socks and grabbed the lightweight blanket on her way back downstairs—the entire time reminding herself not to be impulsive.

He was exactly what she'd look for in someone, ordinarily. He even had several Dominant traits. But that was what she always did—mistake one trait for something else altogether. So what was her goal with him? She questioned herself over and over, trying to talk herself in to—or out of—*something*. But by the time she'd finished, nothing had changed, and she headed as quickly as she could back to the place where she felt completely at peace.

But when she stepped back into the sitting room, the fireplace crackled and a lone cup waited on the coffee table of an empty room. The lights flickered on the tree, and everything was perfect, visually. But her heart sank. She knew this wasn't going anywhere tonight. Or ever. But that didn't change the fact that she wanted every bit of time that the evening had to offer. It was at least six hours 'til daybreak, and as far as she'd been concerned, she'd had until then.

Except there was only her now. The lights outside didn't show anything but the falling snow, and seeing how thick it'd gotten on the ground, she worried if he'd be safe driving home. Did he have chains? It hadn't been snowing when he'd come earlier, so he'd at least need a few minutes put them on. And that meant that maybe she still had a chance to stop him.

Bolting toward the lobby door, she ignored the look she got from Adam and scurried to grab the knob. But before she had a chance, it opened, and Devin came in, shaking off snow and dusting his jacket. When he looked up and saw her there, he took one pass at her attire and back up at her face. "Where were you going?" His eyebrows narrowed as he waited for her reply.

"Nowhere?" she said, earning a deeper frown from him.

They both glanced at Adam—who had probably gotten more excitement in one night than ever before—and silently nodded to each other, heading back to the sitting room and out of his direct view.

Once they walked in, Devin pointed to the coffee cup on the table. "That's decaf, two creams and three sugars," he said, taking off his jacket.

Curling up in the same corner she'd been in earlier, she grabbed the cup and pulled the blanket over her lap. "Thank you."

"So why were you coming outside in your socks right after you changed?" he asked again, grabbing his cup of coffee from the coffee bar and coming to join her.

Torn between lying to appear less ridiculous or telling the truth, she opted for truth. It always ended better. "When I came back down, I didn't see you. I thought you'd left," she said. "I wanted to stop you."

His face softened, and a smile crossed his lips.

"Listen, Strawberry. I know we just met, but here's the thing. I don't lie. I might not always be the most stellar, upstanding citizen… But I won't tell you one thing and do another. And since we only have a few hours left," he continued, "I'd really like to get back to our conversation."

Taking a slow, deep breath, Holly sunk into the couch and relaxed. He really was someone she felt she'd known all of her life. A true, comfy friend. Nothing about him made her feel anything but comfortable.

Reminding herself where they'd left off in conversation, she said, "I think it was my turn last."

"It was. But I think we're ready for deeper conversation. The kind that flows without turns." He winked.

"Okay," she said, thinking this could be fun. "Then let's roll back the clock a little—and share a favorite Christmas memory."

"Your idea," he said. "So you first."

She warmed, thinking back to through all the Christmases past, searching her memory for one that stood out. "The one Christmas morning that I remember the most was shortly after my mom married my stepdad. We'd been kind of poor during the few years Mom was a single mother, so I'd gotten used to going without. It hadn't been a big deal, really," she continued. "I didn't need much, and my mom kept it together the best she could. Anyway, I was seven years old, and I woke up early this particular Christmas morning—I mean, it was-still-dark-out-early. I creeped out toward the living room to see if Santa had come.

"See, some of the kids at school didn't believe in him anymore. My mom said that Santa only visited the kids who still believed, so you can bet your last dollar I'd been determined to believe, making sure I mentioned it to everyone who'd sit still long enough to listen." She laughed as the memories flickered to life.

"As I crept down the hallway, the glow from the lights on the tree grew brighter. I followed their path until I reached the end of the hallway, pausing in anticipation. What if he hadn't come? What if the kids were right? I held my breath and stepped out into the living room, completely stunned at what I saw. There were toys everywhere! In the tree, around the tree, and on the sofa. Dolls, games, and even a little stereo that played cassette tapes! I ran over to the tree and pulled a beautiful Barbie doll off a branch, looked around, and just started crying."

Devin listened to every word as she continued, explaining how awesome her stepdad was and how much he loved her mom. He'd come into their lives and made them better than she could have ever imagined.

"So you're an only child?" he asked.

"Yeah," she answered. "I'm not sure why they never had kids together, but he always loved me like I was his."

"Where are they now? I mean, if that's not crossing our line of anonymity," he said, his eyebrows raised, a smile reaching the corners of his eyes.

"They're in Oregon," she said. "Moved there a few years ago. So what about you, Devin? What's your favorite Christmas memory?"

"Right now, this one's topping the charts."

She smiled in response, but he remained stoic, his eyes fixed on her.

"Can I ask you a question?"

"Anything."

"What I said earlier—about my needs," she clarified. "You didn't seem to flinch. I'm trying to figure out if that was because it wasn't new to you, or if it was just because you have this incredibly gifted poker face?"

Devin smiled. "Maybe a little of both."

"No fair. You can't keep answering in riddles."

Settling back into the opposite corner of the couch, he rested his arm along the back and answered. "I do have an incredibly gifted poker face. But no, it wasn't completely new to me."

CHAPTER 7

DOZENS OF THINGS swirled through his mind as he contemplated what to say next. He should tell her about seeing her earlier. It didn't seem right anymore. But now it just seemed awkward, and making her feel foolish was the last thing he wanted. Maybe because it was Christmas, or maybe not. But he was a goner for this girl. She could ask for the stars, and he'd find a fucking way to get them.

"I don't know much about the lifestyle part," he said, using terminology she had earlier. "I know about some of the activities, but not much more than locker room talk." Not a complete lie, he'd skirted around having to explain his most recent lesson in immersion. "But if you're willing to share, I'd really like to know more. How did you learn about it?"

For such an intimate conversation, he felt surprise at the way her face lit up. She appeared a shy girl on a few counts, but for some reason, she wasn't shy about this—the subject of sex and kink, no less.

"About eight years ago, I was living in Sacramento," she said. "I had just gotten out of college and worked part-time for a small doctor's office. And on the weekends, I sang with a local band."

Devin listened intently as she went on, envisioning her on stage with a mic, now even more aware of the smooth cadence of her voice.

"This guy used to come in to the club sometimes and listen," she said. "He was in his mid-thirties at the time, but I was only twenty-three, so there was a bit of a gap. He was always well-dressed and appeared to have some money, but at the time, I wouldn't have known a Rolex from a Timex, so it really had no impact on me." She paused, and Devin waited for her to continue, very interested in where this was going.

"But what I *did* notice," she interjected, "was the way he carried himself. The way he spoke and walked and even sipped on his drink. He was truly mesmerizing. I'd always thought he paid special attention to me, but I just assumed it was my overactive imagination. Until one night after our performance ended."

She glanced at Devin. "Are you sure you want to hear all this?" she asked. "I could give you the Reader's Digest version, if you'd rather."

"Sweetheart, you've got my full attention."

She blushed and then picked back up where she'd left off.

"Well, anyway, he waited for me to come out, because he wanted to introduce himself. By the time he left, I'd agreed to have dinner with him," she said. "And that's where it began. He was a Dominant, living a lifestyle I'd never before heard of. But I also hadn't even heard of S&M—which most people think of when they think of kink. So thankfully I didn't have any negative associations to overcome. He showed me an entire new world, a world I fit into with ease. We were together for a couple of years, but eventually, it ended."

"Why did it end?" Devin asked, admittedly happy it had or he wouldn't be sitting in the room with her right now, having to adjust his traitorous dick.

"It was always more of an arrangement," she said. "He didn't want me to miss out on living my life. We agreed from the beginning that two years was all it would ever be."

Devin wondered what kind of idiot the guy had been to let her slip away. But then, he had to have some respect for the fact that he'd put her needs over his own. "I'm sorry," Devin said, honestly sorry for the obvious sadness it caused her. "So what happened next?" he asked, truly curious.

"Well, by the time things ended for us, I had entered my career, but I really missed singing. So I reconnected with a few old friends and started singing again, which helped to fill my extra time. I said goodbye to a Dominant/submissive lifestyle and reverted back into the only role I'd ever known, eventually becoming involved in other relationships. *Vanilla* relationships," she clarified. Devin assumed the term was meant for those outside of kink.

"So that's what you meant when you said you

hadn't been true to yourself," he posed, more of a statement than a question. "That you won't settle for a plain—or a *vanilla*—relationship?"

"Yeah," she answered, a subtle look of regret crossing her face. "If I'm going to be true to myself, I need more."

Devin nodded as he thought about everything she'd so openly shared. "I'm flattered you'd share so much of yourself with me," he said then chuckled. "I'm afraid I don't have anything quite as exciting to share."

"No need," she said, shaking her head and pushing back the blanket. "I hope I didn't bore you to tears with all that."

"Not even close." He reflected that life didn't always ask what people wanted before doling out decisions. "My parents split up when I was a teenager, and my mom moved out of state. I stayed behind with my dad, partly because I didn't want to leave my friends," he said, "and partly because I didn't want to lose my status on the high school football team." He laughed at the irony. "I worked at my dad's bar in my off-time and felt like a big shot cause I had a job. Well, anyway, eventually my dad became ill and that high school job became my inheritance. It's a great place," he quickly amended. "But you know…"

"You didn't have a choice," she said, focused on every word he'd been saying.

"Right." Devin smiled. "But who knows? Life

doesn't come with guarantees."

Holly smiled and nodded, and as Brenda Lee and Bing Crosby sang Christmas favorites, their conversation drifted onto a myriad of other subjects. Always skirting the too-personal stuff. He learned a lot about her and the things she liked. They shared their favorite things to do, TV shows to watch, and even where they wanted to one day travel, exactly the way two old friends might.

When the time felt right, Devin asked her what happened to separate her from her date earlier in the evening.

"We went to a private party," she said, her voice growing somewhat quieter. "He'd had a drink here at the bar before we left, but he seemed completely sober. He continued to drink at the party, and then I swear, it was like a switch got flipped. He started making demands of me that were inappropriate and not what we'd agreed on. Finally, someone overheard what was happening, and they stepped in. He became so belligerent that they actually removed him from the residence. He was furious, and I was a mess. Completely humiliated. Thankfully, everyone was really kind, and after I calmed down, a friend gave me a ride back."

"I'm glad I was still here," he said, imagining what could have happened if he hadn't been.

"That makes two of us."

"You weren't worried he'd come to your room?"

Devin asked.

"Oh, he didn't know which room I was in," she said. "I met him in the restaurant." Seeming to ponder something, she added, "I know you probably have all these ideas about this lifestyle. But the truth is, we hadn't agreed to have sex. It wasn't off the table, but he hadn't earned that yet."

Now, he was even more curious about the lifestyle she was describing. But outside of her—and Eve—there wasn't anyone he knew to ask. No one that he knew of was into this stuff. And it didn't sound like something she'd be able to teach him, either. He thought about the guy throwing the flogger earlier. *Someone* had to have taught him.

Setting his curiosity aside, he sat forward, resting his forearms against his thighs and clasping his hands. He had something to say.

Turning toward her, he spoke with total honesty. "I know we've barely had a few hours to get to know each other, but in that span of time, you've completely captivated me. I won't lie. I'm as much a guy as all the ones who've probably disappointed you. And I absolutely hope you find what you need. It's important to be true to yourself," he added. "Don't ever not be. But here's the thing. The guy you came here to see was as much a poser as some of the guys you call vanilla. It seems to me that just because some guy wears a title, it doesn't automatically make him the real deal. I know we won't ever see each other again," he said, hating the taste it left in his mouth, "but I need to at least know that you'll be more careful and not jump into anything without doing your homework first."

Her green eyes sparkled when she smiled, tugging on his heart. He was going to walk out of here and regret it for the rest of his life.

"I promise," she said.

Nodding, Devin stood and glanced out the window. "It's getting pretty late. And it looks like I might have to put the chains on before I head home, Strawberry. But if you're willing to wait up while I go check things out, I'll come back in and say goodbye properly before I leave." He reached for his jacket and pulled it on, watching her hop up, eyes wide.

"Oh..." Her tone was laced with disappointment. "I...uh...yes. I'll wait right here," she said, offering a smile that didn't reach her eyes.

Pulling on the beanie and then the gloves, he ignored the guilt tightening around his chest. "You've honestly made this the best Christmas I can remember having. But if I stay," he admitted, lifting his gaze and holding hers. "I won't be able to let you keep the promise you made to yourself."

He turned without looking back and headed out to the truck.

IT COULD HAVE been a punch to the gut, the way she

felt the air escape her lungs when the door closed behind him. His words echoed in her mind, weakening her last defense. If she hadn't shared all that with him, he wouldn't be leaving. Because he was doing it to honor *her*. And that only made her regret it all the more. Everything about this Christmas weekend had done a one-eighty.

Holly watched as he walked out to his truck where she saw the cab light come on. She could see that it wasn't snowing anymore when the light from a flashlight flickered to life and Devin walked around the truck checking things out. Quite a bit of snow covered the ground, and though she didn't know the first thing about driving in it, she had a fleeting thought that maybe it was too deep for him to drive in. Maybe he'd have no choice but to stay.

She walked to the window in the sitting room and touched the cold glass. The reflection of the crackling fire and twinkling lights of the tree flickered behind her own. He was out there; she could see him in the shadows. But soon, he would be gone and everything about tonight would be gone with him.

Why was life so fucking unfair sometimes? She swallowed against the knot in her throat and willed away the tears burning the backs of her eyes. This was ridiculous, she told herself. He'd be a great friend, no doubt. He'd probably even be a great lover. But she wanted more. No, she *needed* more. Someone who could satisfy more than just her unique sexual needs.

Someone who'd be willing to take on the role of leader, protector, mentor—and disciplinarian. That was a term she and Devin never even got into. But that's what made her feel free. That's what had been missing over the last few years. And she'd become disappointed yet again, finally deciding that it was time she looked in the right places for what she truly needed.

And now, she stood staring out the window at what her heart mistook as someone she could have had a future with. Her hand lifted to touch her lips as she remembered how it'd felt when he'd kissed her. How that moment had shifted their pretend friendship into a place she hadn't expected to go. Hadn't wanted to go.

But had, all the same.

He'd displayed on so many levels the characteristics of a Dominant. But the fact was, he wasn't one. And that wasn't something she could change. Hell, she didn't even live here. She didn't know anything about his life, what he did for fun, or even if he had kids. They'd agreed to bypass all that stuff.

And now, he was leaving.

There was too much complication in her life to make this work, even if he'd be willing to learn. No, she couldn't see this going anywhere beyond this single night. She'd see him off and head upstairs where she'd spend the rest of the night alone. At least things were ending better than if Devin hadn't been in the restaurant at all.

A shiver ran through her when she remembered the way her date had behaved. He was no Dominant. And the first thing she intended to do was to get online and warn off any other unsuspecting submissive girls. That guy might know the technicalities of being a Dom, but he didn't live them. This had been a good lesson, one she wouldn't soon forget.

When she saw the flashlight go dark, she strained to watch for Devin, finally catching him moving up the path toward the front of the lodge. Without even realizing it, she padded over to the lobby door and opened it herself, paying no attention to what Adam was doing behind the front desk. Devin came through, patting his hands against his now wet pants and coat.

Guiding her away from the entryway, he pulled off his gloves and turned her to face him, resting his hands on her upper arms. "Since we've been open and honest with each other all night and we'll never see each other after tonight," he began, looking intently into her eyes, "I have something to say." He paused, and she waited on bated breath. "I may not hold the title of Dominant. I may not even be the kind of guy who could. But you opened yourself up to that asshole, and he wasn't what you thought, either. I'm about to walk out of here forever, and there's just one thing I want answered."

She searched his eyes, moving from one to the other, silently begging for something she couldn't name.

"What?" she asked, her voice cracking as a single tear escaped and slid down her cheek.

DEVIN WATCHED HER fight back tears, never more aware of a connection with a woman as in this moment. Brushing away the renegade tear, he asked the only questions that mattered.

"If you hadn't made yourself that promise, would I be taking you up those stairs right now? Would you be in my arms and following my lead within the next passing minutes? If you hadn't made yourself that promise, would you have given me the chance to make you mine?"

Tears welled in both of her eyes now as she sniffled and opened her mouth, but said nothing. Devin waited, searching her expression for the truth he hoped she'd give. After licking her lips and taking another breath, she simply nodded.

It was genuine and raw, and it made his chest hurt. What the fuck was he doing here still? He needed to let her go. Wasn't it enough that he had to pummel her with questions to satisfy his own ego?

"Thank you for being honest," he said, suddenly aware of their proximity to the front desk.

Pulling her close, he pressed a kiss against her forehead and breathed in the scent of her hair one more time before stepping back and holding her gaze. "I'll never forget you, Strawberry," he whispered.

"Ditto, Superman," she said, her voice strained.

"Come on," he added, wondering where Adam had disappeared to. "I'm walking you to your room. You don't need to be down here alone."

She didn't reply, only followed, dabbing a tear and nodding her head.

HOLLY ALLOWED DEVIN to lead her up the staircase to her room. It was better this way, she told herself. Better than standing at the window, watching him get into the truck and leave. It already felt like she was losing more than a friend, and all she wanted now was to curl up into bed and cry.

What was the matter with her? This couldn't go anywhere—for far more reasons than the simple fact that he wasn't a Dominant! There was too much chaos in her life to subject anyone else to, anyway, she rationalized as they reached the top of the stairs.

"What room number?" he asked.

"Nine. The last one on the left."

"Where's your key card?" Her heart sunk as she pulled it from her bra and handed to him. Would he kiss her goodnight? Or would he just be on his way?

Slowing as they arrived, he turned her to face him, pressing her back against the door.

Devin took her face into his palms while his deep blue eyes pierced into hers. "I forgot one question." He rested his forehead against hers, his breath becoming a part of her own. "Had you been planning on hooking up with that asshole tonight?"

Totally confused and equally embarrassed, she wondered why he was asking, but answered anyway. "Maybe," she admitted, choking on her words.

"And once you found out his true colors, would you have walked away?"

"Yes," she whispered again, sickened at the whole mistake.

"Fuck it," he whispered, as if more to himself than to her. Meeting her eyes, his words were crisp and full of demand. "Then you can walk away from me, too." His lips crashed across hers, hungry and powerful. She opened and met him with needy strokes in return, granting him silent permission. He took what he wanted, and it was familiar. Something about it seemed so familiar.

Home. That was the only word that came to mind as he slowed and looked into her eyes once more, searching them one at a time.

"But you have to say yes," he said, his eyes full of hope and lust.

She didn't have to think about it. The answer had been there all night. *Yes.* She knew it would end by the morning, but there was no point in denying them both what they so badly needed now.

"Yes," she whispered into his mouth, closing her eyes and offering herself.

"Good answer," he said, nipping her bottom lip,

teasing and tasting her with a kiss that started slow and became urgent, making her sex ache for more. An ache that had been there for hours—an ache she'd ignored. Until now.

The door clicked, and moved behind her, sending her pulse racing. She stood frozen as he held her gaze, perhaps waiting for her to make the next move. Slowly, she began to step backwards, intent on not losing sight of the deep blue gaze that calmed her fears and felt like home. The door closed behind him as they cleared the threshold, and he stilled, sending her heart into a rapid staccato.

"I'll wait here while you use the restroom if you need to," he said as he removed his jacket. "And, Holly…" He paused to look up. "Relax."

CHAPTER 8

THE BATHROOM SUGGESTION had been good, and after she finished, she freshened herself up, using the toothbrush and a cold washcloth on her face. Her nerves were lit, and she couldn't understand why. She'd learned to be confident in her sexuality quite some time ago. But something about Devin made her nervous. The kind of nervous she hadn't felt in years.

Maybe because it was somewhere around two AM on Christmas morning following one hell of a plane ride and a date-gone-terribly-wrong. Or maybe the many hours of deep conversation or the jacked-up situation waiting for her when she got home did it. Or maybe it was just something about *him.*

After a quick look in the mirror and then at her clothes, she laughed.

Real sexy.

She had nothing in the bathroom to change into, but under her clothing, she still wore the red lingerie that no one else's eyes had ever seen. Hopefully, Devin liked red lace.

When she came out, he sat in a large chair, his legs relaxed and his arms casually resting along its sides.

She padded forward and stopped, not knowing what to do next, reminding herself that this was one reason why she preferred a D/s relationship. She didn't need to do the thinking. She didn't need to be in charge. She only needed to be willing, and someone else took the helm.

But for tonight, she could do vanilla one last time. Preparing to approach him and lead them onto the bed, she—

"Look, I don't know what to call this," he said, interrupting her thoughts. "I know this ends with tonight, and I don't expect anything beyond that. And I understand and respect the promise you made to yourself, but here's the thing." He stood and moved toward her. "I refuse to call this a hook up."

His tone was sincere as his eyes bore into hers, reinforcing his words. "That's *not* what this is." He paused, coming even closer, sending her heart racing all over again. "Not for me. But I'll regret it for the rest of my life if I don't feel your warmth beneath me at least once. Touch you the way I've been aching to do all night. Kiss your lips the way I've craved for the last several hours, and watch your face when I make you come for the next several hours."

Holly's breaths came quick and shallow as her heart raced. Right now, he could call it anything he wanted, because she was totally his.

His eyes darkened, and he spoke softly into her ear. "This is two old friends," he whispered, creating a rush of goosebumps. "Unashamed. Not judging. No pressure. No BS. Just two friends sharing a Christmas night."

Holly inhaled deeply, willing herself to relax as his words swirled around her like a thousand feathers tickling her flesh. He lifted and cupped her chin as he kissed her again, only this time softer. It teased and taunted as he licked and moved away, nipped and backed off. He braced her at the small of her back, pulling her into him in a possessive move. Everywhere his lips brushed left a wake of goosebumps. She noticed when the hand holding her chin slid down and grasped her neck, gently squeezing the sides. She gasped, even though her airflow was unaffected. The pressure he applied felt threatening, yet wasn't. She liked this move. His show of dominance. Maybe he'd seen it somewhere, or maybe it was just how he was. Whatever the case, it was more than working.

And it more than made her wet.

As if waiting for her expression to declare her consent, he remained in place, watching her closely.

"Do you trust me?"

Despite knowing she could readily breathe, she enjoyed the sensation he was creating for her. A feeling of helplessness, which by now he could tell she wanted. But the question remained, *did she trust him?*

She nodded. She did.

Smiling, he gently walked her backwards, one hand resting on her throat, the other bracing her back.

When the backs of her knees hit the bed, she stopped, still drowning in the darkened blue gaze focused completely on her.

Pressing her down, he guided her onto the mattress with the hand at her back. Once he had her where he wanted, he climbed up, framing her face with his hands. Hovering over her, he lowered his lips to kiss her forehead and smiled. The dark t shirt he wore stretched as the muscles in his arms flexed when he moved. Suddenly having an urge to touch and see his chest, she brought her hands up to his shoulders—where he stopped her.

"Not yet," he said, teasing. "Me first."

Both frustrated and aroused, she let her arms fall back down and grabbed at the sheets by her sides while he continued his taunting assault. The nips at her ear left a trail of goosebumps as his warm lips worked their way down her neck. Focusing on the front of her throat, he gently kissed and bit her there.

Unable to stop the moan that escaped, she writhed in the bed as the throb between her thighs grew into an ache. It'd been a while since she'd last had sex, and she was thankful that she'd never gotten intimate with the fake Dom she'd come to town to see.

Banishing those thoughts, she focused on Devin and the way he nipped at her throat, making her even more desperate. His hands roamed her body, running along the length of her legs, over her yoga pants and upward, coming to rest atop her t shirt, between her breasts, leaving her gasping for air.

Lolling her head back and closing her eyes, she moaned again while he kissed downward over her breasts, taking her nipple between his teeth, right through her thin t-shirt. Attempting to satisfy some of her growing need, she rubbed her legs together, hoping for friction near her sex.

"Oh no, you don't," he said, pausing in his exploration over her clothes. Her eyes shot open, and he smiled that wicked-as-sin smile. "Better stop wiggling if you want what I think you want."

In a snap, she breathed in deeply, forcing her body to quell just as he bit and released her nipple.

"Ahhhh," she yelped breathlessly. His capable hands acquainted themselves with her every curve. He squeezed her ass and then her thigh. Sweeping up across her pussy and over her mons, he left her in goosebumps. His hand came to rest again on one very heavy breast where he kneaded and squeezed, making her whine in desperation.

"Please, Devin," she whispered, in aching arousal.

"Please, Devin?" he toyed. "Oh, I'm taking my time, sweetheart. You just need to learn some patience."

"Oh god," she said breathlessly, fighting wiggling and writhing beneath him.

He tangled his hands into her hair. "Fuck, you're so beautiful," he whispered, his eyes dark with hunger. "But this needs to go."

Within a moment, he'd pulled her t-shirt up and over her eyes, and she lifted her head and arms for him to slide it the rest of the way off. He pushed himself up with his hands and stared down at the lacy red bra she'd poured herself into earlier.

"Gorgeous." He tugged one cup down to expose a beaded nipple.

"Oh God," she whimpered, watching the way he lowered his face to drag his tongue across it. Then he blew against her wet flesh, making her shiver. "Fuck." He lifted up onto his knees and grabbed the tops of her yoga pants to tug them down and off.

He stood, looking at her in nothing but the red panties and bra. With both hands, he grabbed the back collar of his shirt and pulled it over his head, revealing his strong chest and thickly muscled abs, making Holly catch her breath. He was cut. The tight muscles of his arms contracted as he tossed the shirt aside, causing her to swallow and yearn to run her hands over him.

Then she slid her eyes down his happy trail and watched anxiously as he unsnapped his pants. Slowly, he opened the fly and then paused. Her eyes darted to his as her anticipation grew. Why did he stall?

A sly smile crept across his face as he studied her. "You naughty girl," he toyed, and heat filled her cheeks. "I think I'll make you wait." He tucked himself back in before she'd even had a chance.

What the hell was wrong with him? He was acting

like a Dominant, and this was always the part she hated. "Devin," she begged, playing the role. "Please, I need you." Arching her back, she pushed out her breasts, wiggled, and moaned in need. But he shook his head.

"Sweetheart, I know exactly what you need," he said, sending a rush of adrenaline through her body. "Besides my poker face, I failed to mention I'm also a quick study. And you," he said, lifting her hands above her head and bending near, "wear your heart on your sleeve."

WHEN HE'D STARTED with her, he'd worried that he wouldn't know how to please a girl like Holly. But it hadn't taken long to see the way she responded to him naturally. So rather than try to be someone he wasn't, he went with the idea that he was good enough, as is.

Before she could question him, he pulled her panties down and around her ankles. Then he pulled the other cup of her bra down, exposing both of her breasts, liking the idea that her clothes were still on, but not helping hide her bits.

He pushed her feet up onto the bed and parted her knees, so fucking ready to plunge inside her creamy bare pussy. But he had plans first.

A groan escaped her lips, but she held still and left her arms above her head, making him rock-fucking-hard. As his eyes descended upon her pussy, he had the inclination to slap it. The thought stopped him in his tracks, as it always did—until he remembered seeing that done at the party earlier. His eyes met hers, and he thought about it for a minute. The thought seriously giving him pause. What did that make him if he actually got off from hurting a girl?

Deciding not to go there, at least not now, he reached between her legs and lightly touched her outer lips.

Holly opened her mouth and breathed in, a wanton look washing over her face, and he knew what she wanted.

"Are you wet, Strawberry?" He pressed between her lips until the wetness coated his fingers. He smiled as they held each other's gaze. "I'd say so," he said, swirling his fingers through her creamy middle, growing even more hungry.

He circled her clit a few times, noting the way she reacted and keeping tabs on what she responded to the best.

"Close your eyes, baby." His fingers stilled until she complied. "Relax," he said, pushing into her swollen opening with a finger and caressing the smooth walls. As the seconds ticked by, she relaxed, and he felt her muscles give way. Adding a second finger, he did the same until her knees widened even more, giving him better access.

After moments of gentle coaxing, she was dripping wet and ready, so he plunged both fingers as deeply into her as they would go, causing her eyes to shoot open.

"Huhhhh." She breathed out a rush of air as he assaulted her pussy. Plunging in and out in perfect speed, he made her body shake with each stroke, and her breathing increased to the point of a long uttered cry.

Devin turned his wrist upward and flicked the inside spot that would no doubt send her over the edge. When her whimpers became cries, he slowed down and removed the panties from her ankles with his free hand. Her legs fell open, and without removing his hand from her sweetness, he settled between her thighs, earning another longing moan from her delicious mouth.

"You're beautiful," he said, spreading her lips open as he got up and personal.

"Oh my God, Devin," she cried. "Please fuck me already!"

He laughed and instead swept his tongue between the folds of her flesh, tasting her for the first time. "Oh God, you're sweet." He lapped at her folds, flicking against her clit and enjoying the way her body shuddered every time.

"I can't take it," she cried.

"Yes, you can."

"Oh God, I'm gonna come!" she said, her body writhing to his touch. And that was all he needed to hear. Concentrating on that hard little nub, he teased and swept across it with rapid fire, holding her hips in place as she came up off of the bed.

She cried out, and he felt the muscles of her cunt suddenly convulse and throb, each wave matching her cries as she came. He lapped up every bit of what she gave him, flicking that little nub again, making her cries even louder. Her thighs came up around his head, and he pushed them back down with his hands, making her scream out one last time.

She panted in exhaustion, and her gaze found his. He knelt upright on the bed, and when he began to undo his pants, her eyes drifted to his hands once again. Only this time, he took out his cock and held it for her to see. He didn't suppose he was any kind of cock-god, but he knew he was no lackey, either. When her eyes grew wide in appreciation, he smiled.

Freeing it completely and slipping his pants down, he pulled the condom from his pocket and slid it on. "Open, baby," he said, glad now he'd decided to get the condoms from his truck when she'd gone up to change.

She drew her knees upward and opened for him, taking her bottom lip into her mouth as she watched him guide his cock toward her waiting pussy. "That a girl," he said, slipping the head into her wetness, giving him a long needed sensation. "Oh fuuuuuck. You feel so fucking good." He pushed in, and in one thrust, he was sunk, making his balls literally ache.

Her head lolled backwards as she cried out, and he

studied her expression carefully. When her head came forward again, she had that dazed look he always liked to see on a girl. The one that said *I'm yours for the taking.*

She smiled softly, and he lifted her legs into his arms as he began pumping into her, hard and fast. He rocketed her body and buried himself balls deep, over and over again.

Their breaths came rapidly, and sweat trickled down his back as he took what she offered.

Slowing the thrusts to keep from coming, he leaned forward and slid one finger down to her ass, circling her tight little hole. She gasped as her eyes bounced up, seeking his. When she didn't object, he continued, gathering some of the slickness from their fucking and pressing his finger into her ass as he continued to impale her. It seemed to make her even wetter, so he kept toying with her while rocking his hips and sliding into her depths. He raised slightly, angling his cock to press against her in just the right spot—the combined sensations sending her near the edge once again.

Devin closed his eyes and allowed his own sensations to take over, feeling his balls tighten, and when he thought he might come, he dropped her other leg and used his thumb to rub hard against her clit.

One finger in her ass, another on her clit, and his cock buried in her delicious pussy. She screamed out in ecstasy.

As soon as he felt her orgasm take her, he relaxed

and let his own follow.

"Fuuuuck!" he cried, unable to stop the words or the orgasm as they both came out in a rush. He stilled as his body did what he'd wanted since he'd met her. He released into her warmth, and as their bodies slowed, he climbed up between her legs and bent to kiss her beautiful face.

CHAPTER 9

Catching her breath, Holly's heart raced like she'd ran a marathon. She laughed to herself—maybe she had. She didn't have a name for what happened, but SEX was definitely not a strong enough word. Her legs were jello, and her skin was clammy with perspiration. When had she last gotten a workout like that?

As Devin pulled from her body, she watched the boyish smile she liked so much cross his face. How could someone so innocent-looking do the things that he just did? He pushed himself forward and hovered over her, making her feel protected and adored. He bent to kiss her lips, and a stray lock fell down over his face, sending lingering pulses of desire to her exhausted pussy.

His kiss was slow and deliberate, loving and kind. The kind that told her the things words couldn't. Soft lips gently pulled against hers, and she tasted herself in his kiss. He leaned his forehead against hers and spoke softly. "Thank you, Strawberry. You have no idea what that meant to me."

"Thank you, Superman," she whispered back,

thinking he really was some kind of superhero.

"Stay put," he commanded, sitting back and tugging up his pants. He climbed off the bed and she watched as he disappeared into the bathroom and out of her sight. Her mind swirled around what had just happened. That was the most *un*-vanilla, vanilla-sex she'd ever had. The entire event made her question herself all over again.

"No," she whispered to herself aloud. "Don't."

She adjusted her bra and ordered herself not to question what she'd already decided. There was no willy-nillying around this time. Things in her life had become out of control, and this was the one way she knew would help to realign everything. Keep her sane.

She heard the water turn off in the bathroom and watched as Devin came out, carrying a washcloth. As he neared, she swung her legs toward the side of the bed, but he stopped her.

"Let me," he said, pushing apart her knees and giving himself access to her well-used pussy. Despite being a little embarrassed, she opened for him as he gently soothed her aching sex.

"Where'd you learn to do that?" she asked, noting the similarity in the act of aftercare.

He cocked his head at her in confusion. "Wet a washcloth?"

She smiled and reached down to take it from him. "No, bring one to your partner following sex."

"I'd tell you, but then I'd have to kill you," he

teased, giving her a wink. Then he laughed openly and said, "I didn't know it was a 'thing,' but if it earns me brownie points, I'll make a note of it."

Pushing herself up to sit, she smiled. "It does."

"Good to know."

She glanced at the clock and said, "It's almost four AM." Would he leave now? Shag 'em and bag 'em? They both knew this wasn't going anywhere beyond tonight, but how was it supposed to end?

He smiled. "Good. Scoot over. That gives us a few more hours."

Holly's heart sang as he lifted the covers for her to slide into. She watched as he undid his pants and took them all the way off this time. His muscled legs and tight ass earned her appreciation and longing. His cock was still semi-hard, making her wonder if she could go another round. But her sex ached, and that usually meant she better not even try. Any more and she'd be wobbly all the next week. He had a gorgeous body, though, and she longed to be in his arms.

Devin slid in beside her and pulled her body into his, resting her head on his lower arm and draping the other one over her waist. She did love being the little spoon, and they fit together like perfectly matched puzzle pieces.

"Merry Christmas, Devin" she whispered, snuggling into him, appreciating his warmth and care.

She smiled as he kissed the back of her head. "Merry Christmas, Holly."

Closing her eyes, she felt him take her hand into his, and in a moment, sleep claimed her.

SOMETIMES DREAMS ARE the one place where you can work out all your shit, he thought as he slowly came to. He'd been dreaming, but it hadn't really been a dream. He'd spent most the night thinking about everything that'd happened with Holly, determining there was more to discover.

Something she'd asked him early in the evening had been niggling around in his head and had probably been the seed of his dream-induced problem-solving.

"Are there things you hide, Devin?" she'd asked. *"That no one else knows...things that would make them see you differently?"*

At the time, he didn't think so. But that was a lie. One he'd been telling himself for a long time, and one Holly herself brought out in him. He needed *more*. He'd always needed more. A deep desire for things that weren't considered polite. Things that stayed hidden in the depths of your mind and kept there. Things he hadn't identified until now. His sexcapades in high school and college evidenced exactly that. Much like trying to quench a thirst with food. Close, but not the thing he needed.

He should have told her about being at the party. It would have given him an opportunity to tell her that he was honestly interested in learning more about her lifestyle. About what was involved in being a Dominant. Of course, nothing guaranteed he was the right kind of guy for that, but there was only one way to find out.

Somewhere in the night, he'd worked it out in his dreams. He was going to come clean. Tell her about being there and why he'd kept it to himself. She'd opened up to him, and he'd hidden behind a mask without realizing it. Maybe she could introduce him to someone who'd show him the ropes, so to speak.

They'd hit it off so well, and damn, she was a little fucking vixen in the sack—his cock hardened again. They'd woken up after falling asleep, and he'd taken her one more time—raw and dirty, the way he'd caught on she liked. But it had also been sweet, with more kissing and caressing. He loved the way her hands ran down his abs, feeling each one slowly. And then how she'd taken him into her mouth, making him nearly lose his nut before she popped off, letting him come all over her gorgeous tits. And the best part was that she fucking loved it all.

But beyond all that, she did something to him that no other girl had ever before done. She made him feel protective of her in a way he'd never known.

Though set to end this morning, maybe there was a way, after all.

Turning toward her, he reached for her pretty face, only to find she wasn't there.

Devin pushed himself up onto an elbow and stared at the empty side of the bed. Empty except for a red bra and panty set.

She was gone. Quickly, he glanced around the room, noting that she wasn't anywhere in it.

He hopped out of the bed, grabbed his pants, and pulled them on. The suitcase he'd seen on the stand was missing, and no other items of hers appeared anywhere.

He spun around to grab his shirt, where he found a note.

My Superman,

How can I say goodbye? As I watch you sleeping so peacefully, I feel I may know you better than I've ever known another soul. Which makes it such an odd feeling, knowing we were strangers just yesterday—and will be again tomorrow.

Thank you for such an incredible Christmas Eve. There's no question, this one will top the charts forever. (And you don't know it, but I scratched three things off my bucket list...)

But this, I want you to know—my every Christmas Eve will belong to you. Wherever our lives may take us, know that every single year on this day, I'll be thinking of you, the man who almost stole my heart.

Merry Christmas, my comfy friend.

Always your strawberry girl,
~ Jenna

Devin got into his truck, studying the lodge in the daylight while the engine warmed up. What a different place it appeared in the day than in the night. Had it only been twelve hours? The girl now manning the front desk said a pretty strawberry-haired woman had left in a cab an hour earlier. How had he not woken up?

Jenna. Her name was Jenna. Fuck, even that made his cock hard.

Their single night of long talks, snowball fights, and fan-fucking-tastic sex had come to an end. An end they both agreed on. And he was okay with that.

Wasn't he?

He backed out onto the newly cleared road and headed toward home. The thought to drive out a little farther occurred to him. To search for the massive iron gate embossed with giant "C" came to mind. But what would he say? *"Hey, I was here last night for an Eyes-Wide-Shut-party, and oh by the way, can you tell me how to get ahold of the girl in the Santa dress?"*

Yeah, not such a good idea.

He considered asking Kyle, his buddy who owned the lodge, to break the rules and give him her information. But again, that was kind of stalker-esque, not to mention illegal.

No, he'd just head home and forget about her. Forget about the cute way she smiled and her honey-smooth voice. Forget about the way her hair smelled and the way she fit against him. He'd forget about the rebel locks of curls that dropped from her ponytail holder and the way she cried when she came.

Yeah. He'd forget all that.

The ride home in the truck was silent as he wound around the curves into his little town in the mountains. He tried to focus on the day he'd be spending with the Mariano family and how all the little kids running around always made for great entertainment. He thought about Mrs. Mariano's amazing cooking and the way they all embraced him like family, even more so now that his dad was gone.

But his thoughts were distracted.

The wet asphalt flicked off of his tires as he rolled into town. The main roads had been cleared, but the fresh snowfall made Main Street look like a Norman Rockwell painting. The only business that was open was The Mountain Cafe, serving a few people breakfast on this Christmas morning. He slowed when he noticed a strawberry-haired girl come out of the restaurant. She looped her arm through an older man's, and when she turned to look before crossing the street, she smiled. A pretty girl. But not the one he—

It occurred to him in that moment that he'd never be the same. The guy who'd stepped foot into the bad-ass Camaro last night, hoping to get a piece of ass from a hot chick, was gone. And left in his place was someone Devin barely recognized. Someone changed. Someone different somehow. Someone grown-up, maybe. Who knew?

But as he turned onto the snowy path that led to his place, he knew one thing for sure.

No matter where life ever took him, there wouldn't be a Christmas Eve that didn't belong to her. And every year, on this very day, he'd be thinking of a certain strawberry-haired girl in a Santa dress. The comfy friend—who stole his heart.

THE END

If you enjoyed Devin's story, keep reading and allow Gabi and Jake to introduce themselves in an unedited sneak peek of *Safe in His Storm*, Book One in a duet to the Perfect Storm Series!

AUTHOR'S NOTE

The best way to find out about release dates is to sign up for my newsletter! And don't worry about spam or getting too many emails. I hate both! You'll only hear from me regarding upcoming books, sales, or sneak peeks!

Newsletter: subscribepage.com/adelaneynewsletter

I'd also love if you'd follow me on social media or join my Perfect Storm Series Reader's Group!

Facebook: facebook.com/annalisedelaneyauthor
Facebook Group:
facebook.com/groups/PerfectStormSeries
Twitter: twitter.com/ohannalise
Instagram: instagram.com/ohannalise

Please turn the page
For a preview
of
Safe in His Storm

Order here!
annalisedelaney.com/safe-in-his-storm

CHAPTER 1

Valentine's Day

"WHAT THE HELL was I thinking?" Gabrielle Adams muttered as she pushed open the door and darted out into the pouring rain.

In a lame attempt to shield her face from the pelting drops, she threw a forearm overhead and ran, trying desperately not to slip. After fighting with the keys, she finally got the door open, jumped inside, and yanked the squeaky thing shut.

Out of the storm but completely soaked, she dropped her head against the steering wheel and sighed. "Ugggh. You *knew* this was a waste," she lectured herself for conceding to yet another blind date.

What a douche this one had been. Brad. Or wait…was it Brant? Geez, she couldn't even remember the swaggy guy's name.

Thank God she'd insisted on driving herself tonight despite her best friend's attempts to convince her otherwise. Josie Mariano knew her better than anyone and probably didn't want Gabi backing out of the latest double date she'd arranged. And she hadn't backed out.

Well, not really.

Feigning a headache might have been cliché, but at least it gave her an excuse to leave. She couldn't handle a single minute more of Josie's date's political commentary or his friend's endless chatter about his all-time favorite subject—himself.

Gag.

Ever since Josie's thirtieth birthday, when she'd started talking about moving out and off the mountain, Gabi's world had shifted off-kilter. They'd become roommates right out of high school, and she wasn't sure when she'd become so dependent on her best friend and housemate. At twenty-nine, she also knew it was past time they each starting living their own lives.

Of course, Josie's interpretation of that translated into finding Gabi a boyfriend. "Time to knock the fucking dust off!" her friend had so eloquently put it. She'd gone along with it, but deep down, Gabi knew the solution lay somewhere else. And even though she passed no judgment, she just didn't subscribe to the boyfriend-of-the-month club the way Josie did.

The incessant tapping of raindrops hitting the car's roof sent a chill down her spine, pulling her from her wandering thoughts. Sitting up, she shook off the angst and started up the car, suddenly aware of how cold it was. How cold *she* was. She reached for her jacket and realized that in her haste to leave, she'd left it inside O'Hooligans.

Well, crap.

Refusing to go back into the bar to retrieve it, she cranked up the heater to full-blast. Too bad she'd be halfway home before the darn thing blew anything more than cold air.

The rain fell in sheets as she wound around the familiar curves of the mountain roads while her car rattled and shook with every pothole it hit. Hating the rain and envisioning a hot shower, her sole focus was to get home, wash the day away, and warm up.

And she could really use a good night's sleep after all the crappy ones she'd been having the last few weeks. Her bad dreams had recently made a bold return, hijacking buried memories and turning them into a three-ring nightmare set on repeat. Never enough information to fill in the missing parts—only enough to cause bile to burn in her throat and panic to course through her veins as they jolted her awake.

What's worse was they weren't only haunting her sleep now. The recent days had become tainted with flashbacks, paying little respect to all the effort she'd put into silencing them over the years.

Why couldn't she just be normal? Her single wish had been to feel safe and live a regular life, something she would have been robbed of even recognizing had it not been for Luc and Sherry Preston all those years ago. In fact, she might have been robbed of *everything* if it hadn't been for them. Since then, nearly every decision she made was with that in mind.

As she neared the next curve, something caught her eye through the frantic motion of the windshield wipers. She squinted, trying to see better, when—

THUMP!

Thrust into a spin, she hit the brakes on impulse and turned the wheel, trying to remember how to pull out of it. She was opposite the cliff's edge, and all she could envision was being sent over the side. Everything moved in slow motion as her heart raced and body froze. Without knowing what to do, she squeezed her eyes shut and held on with an iron grip.

Then, as quickly as it all began, everything came to a sharp, silent stop.

Heart pounding, breath held, she sat immobilized. And except for the heavy drops falling from above, all was still and quiet. Her car must have stalled because not even the soft hum of the motor could be heard.

Gradually, she released the breath she'd been holding and opened her eyes. Her car's headlamps illuminated raindrops as they fell solidly in front of her, but then her gaze fixed onto something ahead. An older pickup, maybe only fifteen feet ahead, was pulled onto the shoulder facing her.

The shoulder!

She was perched on the wrong side of the road, but luckily still on the shoulder and feet away from the edge! *Thank God!*

Gabi shuddered as she processed what had just

happened and tried to imagine how she'd done a three-sixty without either hitting the truck or being sent over the edge into the valley below.

Swallowing against the knot in her throat, she felt a pain in her chest and glanced down, relieved to see that it was only the seatbelt, which was locked and practically cutting her in half. With effort, she pried her fingers from the wheel and reached down with shaking hands to release the buckle. Her body relaxed as she removed the restraint, and she inhaled deeply, taking a moment to collect herself.

Eyeing the empty pickup, she looked around and wondered where its passengers might have gone. It was doubtful they'd have any cell service on this stretch of the mountain during a storm. With it pitch black outside, walking would be dangerous, if not stupid.

The truck was unfamiliar, which didn't really mean anything. Even though the town's population was small, she didn't have the goods on every single person in it. She would drive slower and keep an eye out for anyone she saw on foot as she continued toward home.

Gabi pulled in a thankful breath and turned the key.

Click, click, click.

Her pulse picked up as she tried the key again, without luck.

Crap! Why did her car have to act up now?

She reminded herself she wasn't too far from her cabin, and even in a rainstorm, this was home. She knew most everyone who lived around here, and if nothing else, she was at least safe in her car. Absently reaching back to feel around for her jacket, she cursed when she remembered for a second time she'd left it at the bar, wishing now she'd gone back in after it.

Mustering her courage, she opened her car door and clambered out into slippery mud. The cold wind howled, and the rain came down sideways, immediately re-soaking her. Shivering, she called out, "Hello? Is anyone here? Hello?"

When she heard no answer, she made her way to the truck and peered inside, confirming it was empty and noticing its flat tire. She glanced around once again but saw no sign of anyone.

Hurrying back to her car, she looked toward the road and spotted a tree limb. That must have been what she'd hit. Concerned that someone else might share the same fate, she veered away from her car and headed toward the road. With freezing fingers, she dragged the branch off to the side while the rain and wind continued to batter her face and body.

Great, now she was not only soaking wet and freezing, she was also muddy. *You knew you should've stayed home.*

She made her way back to her car, kicked off the mud as best she could, and slid in. She wiped her hands on her jeans and pushed her sopping hair back from her face, wondering what exactly a drowned rat looked like.

After weighing her limited options, she decided she'd rather stay put in her car, cold and soaking wet, than to try and walk the couple miles in the pitch black and pouring rain.

Just for kicks and giggles, she tried her cell phone. *Of course, no service.* She locked her doors, turned off her headlights, and sat shivering in her seat. After imagining what Luc would tell her to do, she reached up and hit the hazard lights.

What a giant fail the entire evening had been, but Gabi only had herself to blame. She should have known better than to agree to a blind date. As it was, Josie's taste in men tended to be loosely based on her current choice in books, movies, or sports. In fact, her flavor of this month probably only had another week or two at best, Gabi speculated. That girl went through boyfriends like a wedding went through cake.

Either way, she wasn't doing this again, and that was final.

Her clothes were glued to her skin, making her colder by the minute. Leaning her seat back, she curled into a ball in an attempt to get warm. Josie wasn't supposed to be coming home tonight, so she wouldn't pass by and see Gabi's car. Maybe the truck's owner would return with help.

To keep her mind from drifting, she imagined the hot shower waiting for her once she finally did get home. Then she thought about the March wedding she was planning and mentally went over her checklist. She even thought about the wedding set for midsummer, friends of Sherry and Luc's. She'd been thrilled at the referral and was determined to make it perfect. Sherry and Luc were like family, and any friend of theirs deserved the very best she could give.

As she sat trembling in her seat, Gabi ignored the one sound she hated more than any other. She tried to keep her mind off of the constant tapping of the rain and on good things instead.

Anything else was a recipe for disaster.

JAKE THORNTON SILENTLY cussed himself out as headed back to the spot where he'd left his old truck. He should've known better than to drive these mountain roads without making sure he had flares and at least a damned tire jack on board. Especially in a fucking storm.

He'd swerved around a massive fallen tree, narrowly missing it. But he hadn't missed the boulder that had left his Chevy with a flat about a quarter mile back. He'd continued to his cabin on foot, intending to leave the truck there until morning, but the idea that someone else might come along and hit that tree had him digging around in the shed for more flares. In the dark. Because of course, the power had to have gone out, too.

A last minute feeling of guilt had been what caused him to dig around further and find the tire jack, too. As long as he was going to get wet, he might as well change the tire and bring his old girl home. Because any other reason to be out in this mess was asinine.

What a fun trip this was turning out to be.

He'd been coming here a few times a year, every year, for the past ten. Except for the last. Last year, he'd been busy burying his wife. It had been the worst twelve months of his life, and he was ready to bury that, too. Hanging on to what was never coming back was foolish, and he knew it. But try telling that to his heart.

Lisa had meant everything to him. Ever constant, she'd been the one place he'd found true balance. God, he missed her. Beautiful. Strong-willed. And submissive—only for him. One of the most difficult factors in grieving for her was that there were only a handful of people who understood, or even knew about, their relationship dynamic. The thing that uniquely tied them to one another.

Everyone else had no idea. And why should they? It was none of anyone else's damn business anyway. He didn't care how the fuck they lived, and they shouldn't care how the fuck he did.

But he hadn't just loved Lisa; they'd shared a connection few people had the courage to ever experience. Opened up to each other in ways most people would never have the balls to do.

His job had been to take care of her in every way he could, and in exchange, she offered him everything she had to give. She trusted him, without reservation, to care for and protect her.

But he'd failed. So when she died, he died, too.

His weekend here this year was not without purpose. It was time to say goodbye. Peaceful, secluded, and quiet. Jake could think of no better place to put him in the right mindset to let go of the past than here.

He was done grieving. He wanted to live.

There was no false hope of finding someone else he'd connect with on that same level, and he knew he'd never love another woman again, but he could at least let go of what wasn't coming back. This is where he would close the door on this chapter of his life. And slowly open the next.

Instead, here he was trudging through the mud in a bitch of a storm to change a tire in the fucking dark. Soaking. Fucking. Wet.

Wasn't this nice? He scoffed at the laugh Lisa would have gotten out of this. Shit, she was probably orchestrating it.

When he rounded a curve, flashing hazard lights caught his attention, and Jake shielded his eyes to focus through the rain. Facing his truck, a second car was pulled onto the shoulder with its flashers on. *What the hell?* He picked up his pace, and as he neared the vehicles, he didn't see any visible damage or signs of an accident from the back of the car. He made way around to the driver's side window to peer through the fogged up glass.

A veil of blonde hair was the first thing to catch his eye, right before his gaze settled on a wet t-shirt and the terrible job it was doing concealing what was underneath. Two small, perfectly shaped breasts were snugly wrapped in the wet material. And, by his estimation, she was freezing. What was she doing parked here? And where in the hell was her coat? It was a damn winter storm! He wondered if someone had hurt her, and the thought abruptly infuriated him. His gaze drifted back to the erect nipples behind her rain-soaked shirt—and he corrected himself. God, what if something had happened to this poor girl, and he's lusting after her tits?

But how *had* she gotten so wet? Ten different scenarios buzzed through his head. He looked around but saw no one else, nor any obvious signs of trouble—other than the fact that she was here.

To find out what happens next, order your copy of
Safe in His Storm here!
annalisedelaney.com/safe-in-his-storm